THE SILENCE OF MEMORY

A ROGER AND BESS MYSTERY

M. LEE PRESCOTT

Published by Mount Hope Press

This book is a work of fiction. Names, characters, places, and events are products of the author's imagination or are used fictitiously. Any resemblance to actual people (alive or deceased), locales, or events is entirely coincidental.

M. Lee Prescott's Website and Newsletter Sign-up

For Louise and Winward, with love

Chapter 1

As the rooftops of the village came into view, she sighed. "It was a lovely honeymoon, thank you." The jeep left the tree-lined parkway, both sides a blaze of green and early fall colors, and Bess leaned over and rested her head on his shoulder.

Roger kissed the top of her head, calmed by her familiar scent of orange and jasmine. "Yes, it was, my darling. Now, back to reality."

Their new home awaited them, completed just a month earlier. They had decided to keep their own residences until they married, so this would be their first night in the house. Bess's cottage was now rented to a new colleague at Old Harbor Friends. At the edge of campus, the cottage was an ideal spot for school employees. Jim Lippicott and his wife, Sally, had been delighted to take it and had already offered to buy.

Roger's condo in Bentley had sold in one day, and the closing was handled by his attorney while they were away. He had packed up and moved everything to the new house just before the honeymoon, as had she. They had made up their bed and unpacked a few clothes, but everything else was still in boxes. He was eager to unpack the studio. Painting in the evenings and on weekends was his relaxation, the way he let go of the horrors of his job. The new house had gorgeous studio space for both of them with plenty of northern light.

Their beautiful home, an updated cottage-style, had been built on Winthrop land, which Bess had inherited from her former fiancé, Harry Winthrop. When Harry's attorneys had contacted her after his murder, she had been shocked to discover that his will left everything to her. She had tried to give it back to his father, Harry Winthrop Senior, but the elder Winthrop had refused and insisted that his only remaining child would want her to have it.

After Roger proposed, it had taken every ounce of her persuasive powers to convince him that they should build on the land. It was different lot than the one where she and Harry had planned to build, but just a short distance away. Harry Winthrop Senior, the village's and school's most generous patron lived less than a mile away and was delighted to have them nearby. Between her almost-father-in-law and herself, they had finally won him over. Roger, hopelessly in love with her for most of his life, had thrown up his hands and agreed.

"Are you happy about the house?" she asked, running gentle fingers through his thick salt-and-pepper hair.

He gazed over at her with a tenderness that nearly broke her heart. "I'm happy that I'm with you, and happy that you're happy. That is more than enough for me."

"Oh, Roger, did we bully you into this?"

"My darling Bess, have you ever known me to succumb to bullying?" He reached over and patted her hand. "Did I not spend hundreds of hours with that goofy architect, Sam Waters, working on the plans? Did I not bully you into the barn, the larger studio, and the den? Did I not tell you that I loved the spot we chose and that I'll be blissfully happy there with you?"

"I know, but I want you to feel totally comfortable."

"Your presence is all the comfort I need." He parked the jeep on Main Street alongside the Tavern and turned to her. "Let's have lunch before we head home, okay?"

"Great idea!" Her green eyes brightened and she smiled the beautiful smile that had melted his heart since they were teenagers.

"I love you, my darling," he said, rough hand caressing her cheek.

"I love you, too."

Bess leaned over and kissed him.

After returning her kiss, he leaned back and patted her knee. "Come on, Ms. Demaris. We don't want to be the talk of the town, making out on Main Street."

CHAPTER 2

Wixie squinted at the figure in the clearing, her glasses lost through a hole in her jacket pocket. What was the person doing? He appeared to be digging a hole. A black bundle lay on the ground nearby. He wore a hood, with something red peeking out of it. The thicket shielded Wixie's presence and she squinted to determine what the red might be. She considered going closer to ask the way to the road and to satisfy her curiosity about the stranger's behavior, but something held her back.

She had run away from her father's and was determined to find her way through the woods to the road on the other side of the village. From there, Mommy's house would be a short walk. Her father, Garrett Rollins, school archivist at Old Harbor Friends, lived on campus, in an apartment in one of the dorms. Since the divorce, Rollins's second wife, Palla Forest, Wixie's mother, now occupied the house they had built at the edge of the village. Wixie hated the apartment, but loved going down to the common room at night, where the boarders would play games with her. Most of the time, they indulged the five-year-old, and they were often called upon to babysit since Wixie's dad was dating again. In fact, Lily, the new girlfriend had practically moved in. Wixie did not like Lily.

The scent of honeysuckle and damp leaves surrounded her and she realized she had forgotten her inhaler. Wixie was allergic to mold and several varieties of plants and trees, especially birch trees, of which there were a number in these woods. Suddenly, she sneezed and the stranger jumped, the hood falling back, his eyes peering sharply in her direction. Without a sound, he ran toward her hiding place and she saw his face, covered in a horrible red-and-black mask.

With a scream, Wixie turned and ran back toward campus, back to Daddy. When she reached the athletic fields, she spied some of the lacrosse players from her dorm and hurried to meet them. She did not look back until the team had surrounded her. When she did, the path was empty, the stranger swallowed up by woods that no longer seemed friendly or inviting.

"Hey, Wixie-bean." Tall senior, Cal Gardner gazed down at the dark-haired child, her brown eyes frozen in fear, tiny body trembling. "What's the matter? Did you see a ghost in there?"

The child shook her head. "It was Spiderman. He was digging a hole. There was something beside him."

"Hey Wix, hold on! What're you talking about? You saw Spiderman? Are you sure?"

Before he could inquire further, the five-year-old ran off, leaving him staring after her, lacrosse stick slapping his calf.

Wixie decided to skirt the campus and walk through the village. Her father and she had walked to Mommy's a few times in nice weather. It was not a long walk. She would be home in time for lunch.

Three hours later, Wixie Rollins had not arrived at her mother's. Her father, having searched the campus and village, called the police and his ex-wife to report her missing.

CHAPTER 3

Pete Dugan walked into the office, waving at Lottie Willis, his boss's secretary. "Hey Lottie? Anything come in?"

"Wouldn't I have called you if it had?" She watched the ruggedly handsome thirty-five-year-old shuffle through papers, his sharp blue eyes serious. The angry scar running across his forehead had faded, but it had altered his youthful looks forever. She often caught their boss, Roger Demaris, staring at the wound, which had nearly killed the young man he loved like a son. Demaris blamed himself for Pete's brush with death, and no therapist or counselor would ever convince him otherwise.

"You're looking especially pretty today, Lot. Hot date?"

The fifty-something secretary, her curly brown hair recently cut and dyed, blushed, pulling the hem of her mauve polyester sweater down over her muffin-topped midsection. "Don't I wish? Have you heard from the boss?"

"Nope, they're on their honeymoon, remember?"

"You're happy for him, aren't you, Pete? I mean, now that it's finally happened?"

Dugan shrugged. He had nothing against Bess Dore, but after watching his boss pine away for her since the day he had come on the job, he remained wary. Glad they were together, he still worried about Rodge. No one knew the boss's vulnerabilities like his assistant. "Mother Hen," Demaris called him, usually with humor and patience.

The phone rang and Lottie picked up. "Regional Homicide Division, Lottie Williams speaking."

Dugan watched her face pale as Lottie looked up at him. "You better take this," she said, handing him the phone.

"Hello, Detective Pete Dugan, RHD."

"Detective Dugan, this is Pru Marsden, headmistress at Old Harbor Friends. I believe we've met?"

"Yes, Ms. Marsden, how can I help?"

"A body was found in the woods near the campus athletic fields. I don't know the details, who it was or manner of death, but I'm calling because we have a missing child who might have seen something, Wixie Rollins. She's the five-year-old daughter of our archivist, Garrett Rollins."

"No one called RHD about the homicide, Ms. Marsden. Missing kids are usually handled by the local police."

"Please, may I speak to Lieutenant Demaris? Mr. Winthrop suggested I call him. He's prepared to call the governor, if necessary."

"The lieutenant's on his honeymoon, but they return today. I'll try to reach him, okay?"

CHAPTER 4

"The newlyweds have returned!" Rachel Ramos, co-owner and Tavern hostess, clapped her hands as she spied Roger and Bess. The restaurant was half empty, the lunch crowd thinning out. "Tilly'll have kittens!" The petite blonde, dressed in wool slacks and white cashmere sweater, came forward and hugged Bess, then Roger.

"Hey, Rach," he said. Better to get greetings over with so they could find a quiet table. He nodded at Charlie Boardman, who stood behind the bar as he led Bess toward a table by the window, knowing full well that news of their arrival would reach the kitchen at any moment.

Sure enough, as soon as they sat, the double doors swung open and Tilly Rogers, Rachel's partner in business and in life, burst out. At six feet, the slender cook with wiry gray hair caught up in a hairnet towered over both of them as she crossed the room in three strides and gave each a bear hug.

"So good to see you both! You're looking well. Lunch's on the house. What'll you have?"

They both ordered Cobb salads and Tilly's tea.

"So, how were the Berkshires?"

"Beautiful," Bess said. "Dreamlike, as the song goes."

"And I hear he dragged you to the yoga place, too."

"It was lovely. A peaceful, spiritual place. I hope we'll return again soon."

As Roger watched his wife, his smile of contentment was not lost on his old friend.

"So, you've converted her, then?"

"Hey, don't look at me. Kripalu is all about listening to yourself. Bess made her own choices."

"I did. Yoga, meditation, some really interesting workshops. We took the most lovely hikes. It was heaven. I'm going to propose that we find a spot for a labyrinth on Old Harbor's campus, or maybe the town council would consent to a labyrinth on the village green. That was one of my favorite things."

Tilly smoothed her soiled apron. "Oh, Lordie! Well, gotta get back to work. Good to have you back, both of you."

Roger leaned forward and took Bess's hand. "This might have been a mistake."

"No, it's fun to see people. We'll be alone tonight, at home." She smiled at him and his heart leapt. He still could not believe he was married to the woman he had loved for over twenty years.

"Glad you feel that way, because Cathy and Lois just walked in."

The owners of the Honeysuckle B and B, also partners in every sense of the word, rushed over with open arms. "Thought you could sneak into town," Cathy Nolan said, hugging Bess as Lois embraced him. Tall and slender, her dirty-blond hair tied back in a haphazard ponytail; Cathy and her partner were dressed in jeans and faded purple Honeysuckle B and B tee shirts.

Lois Arnold, the shorter of the two, stocky with short, dark hair, grinned at him. "We spied you through the window. Congratulations."

"Thanks, Lo," he said, genuinely glad to see his friend. "How's everything in town?"

"Quiet."

"That's what we like to hear."

Bess smiled up at the couple. "Would you like to join us?"

"You sure?" Lois asked, looking from husband to wife.

He laughed. "Absolutely."

"Well, maybe for one glass of Tilly's tea," Cathy said. "We want to hear all about your trip."

The friends sat back and began a leisurely conversation, Cathy and Lois peppering the newlyweds with questions. When they had learned as much as husband and wife were willing to share about the Berkshires, the yoga center, and the past ten days, Lois leaned back in her chair.

"I know I've said this several times before, but finally! So happy for you guys." She clinked both their glasses, but her eyes stayed on him, her friend since grade school. *Time for him to be happy*, she thought.

Cathy observed Bess, who also looked happy. Since her high school love affair with Roger Demaris, the forty-three-year-old art teacher had lost a husband of ten years, then a fiancé. It was clear that she loved Roger and was content, but unlike her husband's, Bess's feelings were tempered by heartache and the fear of losing yet another beloved partner. Before the honeymoon trip, Bess had confided in her friend, telling her that she was seeing a therapist. The therapist was helping her work through her anxiety and fear, helping her let go of the past with Roger, her husband, Macomber Dore, and her recently murdered fiancé, Harry Winthrop.

Bess reached over and took her husband's hand. Instantly, he turned and gave her a gentle smile, the kind that melted icebergs. Roger Demaris was finally with the love of his life. More extraordinary things had happened in Old Harbor, but Cathy could not recall one at present. "So's the house ready?" she asked.

Bess laughed, grinning at her husband. "If you ignore the boxes piled to the ceiling everywhere."

"Lo and I want to see it and bring you a meal."

"Thank you for the offer, but you were both so incredible and generous with the wedding and reception food that we'd love to have *you* for dinner, once we have something to cook with. Thank goodness Roger has a few more days of vacation so we can try to make a dent in the boxes." Lois gazed toward the Tavern's front door. "Don't look now, but I fear the vacation may be cut short. Pete doesn't look like he's here to welcome you home."

Demaris's heart sank as he spied his second-in-command, accompanied by Brendan Stevens, the young officer who had joined their team a year earlier, poached from the village's police department after his work had impressed RHD's head during a previous investigation. Pete's jaw was set in a scowl, his blue eyes grave. Demaris reached over and squeezed Bess's shoulder, then stood and moved to greet his officers, leading them to a quiet corner of the room.

"Welcome back, boss," Pete said.

"What's up?"

"We have a body and a missing kid."

"Who?"

"Body's in the woods near campus. We haven't been out there yet. Locals are handling it, but the school head, Ms. Marsden, called us, said old man Winthrop requested RHD and he's calling the governor."

"Male or female?"

"She didn't say or didn't know."

"And the child?"

"Wixie Rollins, daughter of the school archivist, Garrett Rollins. Was last seen a few hours ago walking in town, but never made it from dad's to mom's house today."

"How old?"

"Five."

"What the hell was she doing walking anywhere alone?"

"We don't know anything, Rodge. I would've gone out to the scene, but I heard you were back and swung by here first. I suspect it'll ruffle fewer feathers if you're with us."

"Wait a second." Demaris raised a finger and pulled out his cell phone, which he had kept off most of the trip, except a brief check each day to make sure his children hadn't called. He listened to the four messages, two from Harry Winthrop

Senior, one from Governor Pamela Franklin, and the last from Chief Ron Wilbur, his former boss at Old Harbor Police Department. All four messages confirmed what he already knew. Regional Homicide Division had been requested and approved, and the local cops would step back as soon as his team arrived.

"Jesus Christ," he said, taking a deep breath as he gazed back at the table and his lovely wife. *So much for unpacking.* Her eyes met his for a brief second and she nodded.

"Okay, let me say my good-byes and we'll head out. Where are Greta and Megan?" he asked, referring to the team's other detective and their forensic pathologist.

"Greta's on her way. Meg, too."

"Okay, call 'em and then check with Tilly and Rachel about the guest house. We might as well set up there again, if it's unoccupied." He referred to the one-bedroom cottage behind the Tavern, where they had set up camp during a previous investigation.

With regret, he returned to the table, their previous, relaxed conversation a distant memory. A pall now hovered, another brutal death obscuring the light. What would they find in the woods, the same woods where young Harry Winthrop had died? And where was five-year-old Wixie Rollins on this sunny fall day, its afternoon shadow already lengthening?

CHAPTER 5

Demaris leaned over the long black bag. A woman lay inside, her face vaguely familiar. Her head was crooked at an odd angle, and she had an angry red line round her neck. "Who is she?"

"Gretchen Parker," Ron Wilbur said. "Lived here for many years. In Northport. More recently, lives—*lived* in Florida and was up visiting her daughter, Vicky Brown. You guys taking over again?"

Pete stepped between the two men. "Just got a call from Megan, boss. They're parking the van. Be here in five."

Demaris reached forward and gently nudged his assistant to the side. "Listen, Ronnie, I didn't ask for this one. Bess and I just got back. I have a week more vacation and was gonna take it to unpack. I was called in by the higher ups and didn't think it was an option to say no."

"Whatever." The chief shrugged, kicking a stick out of his way. "My guys have plenty to do."

Demaris surveyed the area around the body. "Looks like there was a convention here."

"Not my guys. That would be the lacrosse team. They raced in and found her after the kid went screamin' off."

"Any sign of Wixie Rollins?"

"Nope, and we've scoured the campus and all along the route she'd take to get home."

"Are your men still out looking for her?"

"Absolutely. We won't stop till we find her."

"Thanks, Ronnie."

"No problem. This is our town. We look after our own."

"Of course." Demaris nodded and forced a smile. His old boss looked sickly, face bloated and blotchy. Wisps of thin brown hair lay dirty and plastered to his skull. Wilbur looked twenty years older than his forty-five years. At least twenty pounds heavier than on their last encounter, his rumpled uniform looked ready to burst its buttons.

"Well, we'll let you get to it. Come on guys. Let's clear out! That's a golf bag, by the way. One of those things they use to tote their clubs back and forth from Florida, the Bahamas, or wherever the hell they go."

"Thanks, Ronnie."

"Whatever." Wilbur and his three officers grabbed jackets and equipment bags lying at the edge of the clearing and headed down the path toward campus. Demaris watched their departure and said a silent prayer of thanks for his new position. His forensic pathologist, Megan Krieger, passed Wilbur and his officers on the path. She was accompanied by her assistant Bethany Yuan. Both women were laden with bags.

"Thanks for getting here so fast, Meg."

Krieger motioned to Bethany, and they knelt on opposite sides of Gretchen Parker. "Strangulation. Some kind of wire. We'll know more when we get her back to the lab. Don't see any other obvious trauma to the body. What are all these footprints around her?"

"The lacrosse team," Pete said, rolling his eyes.

Demaris turned to his second-in-command. "Speaking of the team, where are they?"

"Waiting in the locker room. Wilbur ordered them to stay."

"Meg, we'll be back in a bit. See if you can give me a rough idea of when she died and anything about where. I doubt she strolled out to the woods, waiting for someone to come along and strangle her."

"Could've been someone she knew?" Pete said. "Maybe they were taking a walk and he or she whipped out the wire and caught her by surprise?"

"Wouldn't she have wondered why he or she was carrying a golf bag?" Stevens said.

"It doesn't look like she was killed here," Krieger said. "What a mess." She waved her hands at the churned-up, muddy earth surrounding them.

"Do what you can, Meg. We'll be back soon."

Pete's cell phone rang and he listened for several minutes, replying in monosyllables, then said, "Thanks." He looked first at his superior, then Krieger. "That was the clinic. Lab's yours. They're sending an ambulance."

CHAPTER 6

The Old Harbor Friends boys' locker room smelled like every locker room from time immemorial. The damp, sweet scent of competing brands of aftershave mingled with the heavy odor of sweat and rubber. The lacrosse team's presence did not improve the aroma as none had dared shower after practice for fear of incurring the wrath of Chief Wilbur or the head of the elite homicide squad. As the three men entered, all eyes turned to them.

"Good afternoon, gentlemen," Demaris said, his eyes slowly connecting with all sixteen. "We won't keep you long, as I'm sure you've got studies. I wonder if I might have a word with Mr. Gardner? Detective Dugan and Officer Stevens will take general statements from the rest of you. Would that be okay?"

A six-foot-two blond hopped up.

"Mr. Gardner, perhaps you could come with me?"

The young man followed him out into the waning light and they sat on a bench at the edge of the deserted fields. Cal Gardner stared down at his flip-flops, waiting for Demaris to begin. Rugged and strong, his knees and shorts were covered with mud, his footwear strangely delicate and out of sync with the rest of him.

"I thought lacrosse season was in the spring."

"Not here. We have a fall and spring season now, even though the spring's the only one that leads to the all-prep tournament.

"How's it going so far?"

"We lost a lot of players last year, so this is a building year."

"Good luck with that. So tell me about Wixie Rollins."

"She's a cute kid, always hangin' around. Toward the end of practice, she came barreling out of the woods looking like she'd seen a ghost. She was going on about Spiderman and how she'd seen him digging a hole. Said there was something beside him. Then, before I could ask her anything else, she took off running across campus."

"Then what?"

"A couple of the guys and I went in to see if we could find what had spooked her."

"How many of the guys?"

"Just a couple at first, but after we found her—the body, I mean—the rest of the team came in for a look."

"Did anyone know her?"

Gardner shook his head.

"Did you or any of the guys touch the body?"

"I felt her neck for a pulse."

"But you didn't move her, roll her over, look through her pockets?"

"No, nothing like that!"

"Okay, thanks, son. You've been a big help."

"Have they found Wixie?"

"Not yet."

"Poor little kid."

Poor little kid is right, Demaris thought as they walked back inside to join the others.

CHAPTER 7

As the three men headed back down the woodland path, deep shadows enveloped them. "Did you learn anything from the rest of the team?" Demaris asked.

When they stepped into the clearing, the cry of a whippoorwill pierced the silence, and unnatural light from Megan's battery-powered lights on stands cast long shadows all round them.

"Nothing except the usual 'my first dead body' stuff," Pete said. "None of them heard what the kid said except Cal."

"They seem pretty shaken up, sir," Stevens added as they reached the others.

"Yes, they would be, of course," Demaris said, turning to his forensic pathologist. "Anything, Meg?"

"From what we can tell so far, she's been dead about six, maybe eight hours. We'll know more when we do the autopsy. The surrounding ground is too much of a mess to tell much."

He nodded. "Still, let's rope it off and get the crime scene team down to comb through the mud. Pete?"

"I'm on it, boss."

As Pete turned away to speak on his cell, Stevens and Bethany began roping off the area with yellow crime scene tape. Demaris watched them, remembering a year earlier when they had done the same thing not fifty yards from where they stood. Then, they had been roping off the ground around the body of his wife's fiancé, Harry Winthrop, who lay still, an arrow through his heart. Maybe they should rope off these woods permanently, he thought, wondering what Bess was doing. Had she driven out to the house, or would she be waiting at the Tavern for his return?

The EMTs arrived and gingerly settled Gretchen Parker on the stretcher. One arm dangled out of the bag until a look from Krieger prompted one of the men to retrieve the appendage. "I'll meet you there," she said and gathered her equipment. "We'll work all night, sir."

"Thanks, Meg. If you find anything we should know about, call Pete's cell or mine. Greta's on her way, too, if you can't reach us."

"Yes, sir," she said, nodding to Bethany as they followed the stretcher out of the woods.

The three men stood alone, silently staring at the ground where Gretchen Parker had lain.

"Crime scene'll be here at sunrise."

"Good. Thanks, Pete. What do we know about Gretchen Parker?"

"Not much. Grew up in Northport and lived there until about ten years ago, when she moved to Florida with her third husband. Has a daughter who lives in town, Vicky Brown. Remember her?"

His superior nodded. "Member of the book club—one of the younger members, as I recall."

Harry Winthrop, Bess' former fiancé and author of a series of mysteries under the pen name of Anne Greyson, had died almost a year earlier in the midst of an Anne Greyson Reader Weekend, organized by Bess and Harry. The members of a local book club had all signed up for the weekend, among them twenty-eight-year-old Vicky Brown.

Pete nodded. "Yeah, she lives at The Glen." He referred to a condominium complex on the edge of the village where he and his girlfriend, Hillary Dobbs, lived. "You remember, her roommate's Suzanna Costa, a fellow book club member. Their condo is in the same building as Hillary and me. Parker was visiting her daughter for a long weekend."

"Has the daughter been notified?"

"Yes, sir," Stevens said. He walked behind them on the path and now drew up alongside Dugan. "Chief Wilbur had one of his men go out."

"Okay, I want to talk to Vicky. Just need to make a quick stop at the Tavern. Brendan, can you start digging up everything you can on Gretchen Parker? When Greta arrives, she'll help you."

"Yes, sir," the younger man said.

Demaris smiled at his most junior officer, marveling at how he had matured in the nine months with RHD. Even in plain clothes, the thin, wiry twenty-three-year-old still looked about fifteen, but there was a quiet confidence about him now, unlike the young man's deer-in-the-headlights look at their first encounter. Stevens worshipped his superiors but idolized Pete. His short hair was now styled like Pete's and as closely as he could, he dressed like his mentor.

Murder changed people, Demaris mused as the three drove into town. Fresh-faced innocence and naïveté vanished in the wake of evil. Finding refuge was essential, if one wanted to stay sane. Demaris wondered if Stevens had found his.

CHAPTER 8

When they arrived at the Tavern, Bess still sat with Cathy. Lois had returned to the B and B, and the room was filling with diners. Bess waved as she spotted her husband, and was relieved to see his eyes brighten when he saw her.

"What's happened?" she asked. Both women stared at him.

"Gretchen Parker's been murdered."

"Vicky's mom?" Cathy asked, her expression stricken.

He nodded.

"She's stayed with us a bunch of times. Such a sweetheart, which is more than I can say for her boorish husband."

"Didn't I hear he'd passed away?" Bess asked, gazing at her friend.

"About a year ago, I think."

"Would that be Vicky's father?" Demaris asked, wondering why he could not recall Gretchen Parker or her daughter.

Cathy shook her head. "No, he died a long time ago, when Vicky was little. I think Parker was her third husband, after Dennis Harrison, but there might have been another one."

"Dennis Harrison, I know that name," Demaris said.

"Big-time developer," Cathy said. "Made millions in a bunch of developments. The last was the one that's just north of Osprey Point. All those McMansions sold for several million, at least."

"Where is he now?" he asked.

Cathy shrugged. "He cashed in and moved south. Not sure where. He was always a world-class jerk. Made millions, lost millions, usually other people's money. Major philanderer, on his fifth or sixth wife. Runs through their money then moves on. Rumor has it he drove his first wife, Angelina, to suicide when he married Gretchen."

"So, she was wife number two?" Demaris asked.

"I think so," she said. "But he had a bunch of affairs long before he hooked up with her."

"Stevens, find out where this Harrison is living and anything else about him, will you?" Demaris then turned to Bess. "I'm sorry, bride of mine. I'll try to get home for some unpacking as soon as I can."

She hugged him. "No worries. Just take care of yourself, please?"

He returned the embrace, then stood back and kissed her forehead. "You take the car home, okay?" She nodded.

As Demaris turned away, he spied Greta Burke at the front door, duffle bag and enormous pocketbook slung over one shoulder. As usual, his only female detective looked as if she had fallen out of bed—wrinkled shirt, flaxen hair tied back in a snarly ponytail, worn jeans and well-broken-in running shoes. She nodded and approached the group.

"Good, you're here, Greta. Let's head over to the guest house. Ladies, see you later." He nodded, then the four of them headed for the back door.

"Yoo-hoo!" Tilly called as they passed the kitchen door. "Here, take this and call over. We'll whip up whatever you need, on or off the menu." Despite their assertions that they would be headed right back out, the tall cook thrust menus in Pete's hands and waved them away. "Just put in the order and we'll keep things warm. I'll be here until after midnight."

"Thanks, Till."

"Guest house is ready—clean sheets, food in fridge and a few snacks in the cupboards. No one's been over in a few days, but I daresay it'll do, unless we've had another squirrel invasion."

The little one-bedroom cottage, furnished simply in antiques and flea market finds, was a quiet getaway, seldom rented except to handle the overflow when the Old Harbor Inn and Honeysuckle B and B were full. It was comfortable and quiet, and delicious food was delivered whenever they called for it. Demaris was still holding out hope that he would eat dinner at home, knowing the chances of that were slim.

Regional Homicide's main office was in Taunton, about forty-five minutes away. Greta lived in Taunton, and Roger's condo had been in Bentley, a ten-minute drive from the office. With the new house, he had become a villager, like Pete. Stevens lived in Northport and Megan Krieger in Providence, Rhode Island, a twenty-minute drive from the village and RHD.

Tilly had provided each of them with a key. When they reached the cabin, Pete used his, wiggling and coaxing the old lock, only to find that the door was unlocked. As he pushed it open, they heard a rustling. "Shit, there'd better not be any squirrels in there. I hate 'em. Nasty rats with fluffy tails."

He reached in and flicked the wall switch, flooding the living room and dining room areas with light. They stepped inside, surprised to spy open bags of chips on the coffee table, a half-full glass of what appeared to be juice beside them. Chips and pretzels littered the love seat and floor, and a trail led toward the galley kitchen separated from the main room by a counter with four stools.

Dugan drew his gun, eyes darting round the room.

Demaris grabbed hold of his arm. "Put that away. This doesn't look like squirrels, and even if it is, you aren't going to shoot any."

He motioned to Stevens and Greta, who crept quietly to the right of the kitchen, where another trail of chips and peanuts led into the bedroom. They skirted the long pine deacon's table that bisected the room, its eight ladderback chairs tucked underneath.

As they reached the bedroom door, a whimper came from within. Demaris came forward, swiftly stepping round his detectives.

"It's okay, Wixie," he said softly. "It's the police and we're here to help you."

CHAPTER 9

After much coaxing, Wixie Rollins finally took Demaris's hand and came out of the bedroom closet. She now sat on the living room's love seat, sipping grape juice out of a tiny carton. He sat beside her, with the rest of the team a short distance away in the kitchen area. Both her parents had been notified and were on their way.

He smiled down at the child. "You've been a very brave girl, Wixie. Do you think you could tell me about what happened in the woods? Were you playing there?"

"I ran away. I don't like it at Daddy's house."

"Where were you going?"

She shrugged, staring down at the floor, sipping her juice. Several drops trickled down her front, and Demaris handed her his handkerchief. She fingered the delicate embroidery, of his initials, stitched by his former condo neighbor, Zoe Stone. Zoe, a fellow artist, had dropped many hints about her interest in him. They had sometimes shared meals or coffee, but nothing more.

"I wanted to get to Mommy's."

"So, you were walking to your mom's house?"

She nodded.

"Do you know the way?"

"Yup, Daddy walks me sometimes. I got tired."

"Can you tell me about what you saw in the woods?"

Instantly her eyes registered fear. She squeezed the juice carton until liquid trickled out the tiny straw. "Spiderman."

"What was Spiderman doing?"

"Digging a hole."

"Was he tall like Pete?" he asked, motioning for Dugan to stand.

She shrugged. "Dunno."

"Could you tell the color of his hair?"

"Red."

"Like Pete's?"

"No, like Spiderman."

"Did you notice his pants?"

Still squeezing the now empty carton, she stared ahead for thirty seconds. "Maybe black?"

"So he didn't have a whole Spiderman suit?"

"No, just his head."

"What about shoes? Was he wearing sneakers or boots?"

"Dunno."

"What about his jacket?"

"Dunno. Maybe brown."

"Did Spiderman speak to you?"

She began to trembling and shaking her head from side to side.

"Okay, sweetheart, that's enough. You're safe now, and your mommy and daddy will be here soon."

As if on cue, the door swung open, and Garrett Rollins stepped aside to allow a thirty something blonde in jeans and a man's flannel shirt to pass by. "Wixie! Oh, darling, Mommy's here!"

"Mommy!" Still grasping the juice carton, Wixie leaped up into her mother's arms.

Rollins followed the blonde, looking sheepish. "Hey, Wix, you gave us quite a scare." He attempted to embrace his daughter, but the mother turned her back on him, so he spoke to Demaris. "Lieutenant, thank you. Where'd you find her?"

"In the bedroom closet."

"How'd she get in?"

"Door was open."

Rollins cleared his throat. "Lieutenant, I'm not sure you've met Wixie's mom, my ex-wife, Palla Forest?"

"No. Hello, Ms. Forest." Demaris extended his hand, which was ignored. "I know your work. You're a talented artist."

"Thank you, officer, but can I take my daughter home?" She turned from him and glared at Rollins.

The archivist returned the glare with one of his own. "Not before I've given her a hug."

"Fine, but then we're leaving." She handed Wixie to her father and faced Demaris. "Lieutenant, I have absolutely nothing to contribute to your investigation into that poor woman's death, nor will you be talking to my daughter again. She's five years old, for Christ's sake. This is what comes from trusting an irresponsible teenager." She thrust Wixie into her father's arms.

Dugan stepped forward, ready to intervene if needed, but his boss waved him back, watching quietly as Rollins cooed over his child.

"What teenager?"

"His daughter, the colossally self-absorbed Becca."

"Shut up, Palla," Rollins said softly. He was struggling hard to control his temper.

"Wasn't Bec's fault," Wixie said. "I sneaked out when she was in the bathroom."

"Is your other daughter with you, Mr. Rollins?"

"She stayed home."

"I mean, does she live with you?"

"Yes. She spends several nights a week with her mom and the odd weekend now and then. After my divorces, both my girls preferred to live in the homes where they were born and grew up. We thought that was best, but this past year Becca asked to live with me, which is fine. Her mother and I cooperate, for her sake," he added, glaring at Palla, who returned the look.

"I know Becca," Demaris said. "How is she?"

Becca's mother, Clarice Wills ran the village's small bookshop, which carried an eclectic mix of fiction and nonfiction, the latter mostly books with a local connection. The shop had a small parlor with tattered but comfortable easy chairs where patrons could pour themselves a mug of coffee or tea and relax with a book. In years past, patrons would often find Becca Rollins stretched out on the floor working a puzzle or playing hide-and-seek with a friend in the stacks. When he worked in town, Demaris often stopped in at the end of the day or over lunch, the warm, musty shop a welcome change from the station.

"She's okay. Took this year off after graduation, but will be at college next year," Rollins said. "She's going to Greenleaf, so she won't be far away."

"Can we please stick to the point!" Forest said. "My head is about to explode. As I said, I have nothing to contribute, and I'd like to get out of here and take my daughter home."

After several slow, deep breaths, Demaris said, "I know this is very upsetting, Ms. Forest, but we will determine who does and does not have a contribution to make. A woman's been k-i-l-l-e-d and we may need to question a number of people, including you. You are free to take Wixie home, but please expect that one of us will be in touch."

As she turned her arresting violet eyes from him to her ex-husband, Demaris noticed streaks of oil paint on the flannel shirt and what appeared to be a leaf tangled in the strands of her hair. He resisted the temptation to reach forward and remove it, but made a mental note of its shape and characteristics.

She thrust her arms out toward Rollins. "Garrett."

He rumpled Wixie's curls and kissed her cheek. "Okay, Wixie-bean. I'll call later, okay?"

Wixie nodded and nestled into her father's shoulder, suddenly in no hurry to return to Mommy. Forest reached forward. "Come on, Peanut. Let's go *home*."

Wixie moved from father to mother without a word and Palla Forest turned and stalked out, banging the door behind her. How could someone who painted such magnificent, joyful landscapes be such a miserable human being? Demaris stared at the closed door, hoping that perhaps it was the stress of the day that had brought on Palla Forest's terrible behavior. Finally he turned back to Rollins, who looked dejected and sad. "If you wouldn't mind staying for just a few minutes, Mr. Rollins, it would be helpful to get your statement."

"Of course." Without asking, he sat in one of the lumpy armchairs, upholstered in faded green chintz, and doubled over, arms on knees, head in hands. In his late forties, Rollins looked like the history teacher he had been until two years earlier, when he had moved into the full-time position as school archivist, a job created and supported by a historical trust set up by Harry Winthrop Senior. Slender and tall, his sandy hair was thinner than it had been the last time Demaris had seen him, but the trademark salt-and-pepper goatee still graced his sharp, angular jaw.

Rollins was known about town and on campus as a player. Ladies of all shapes and sized swooned over him, but Demaris had never understood the appeal. To him, the skinny archivist looked like a dirty old man in the making, someone to whom intelligent, sane women would not give a glance. But then, who could account for taste? He pulled a straight-backed chair over to face the man and sat down, glancing over at his team. Greta and Stevens sat at the counter, backs to them, working on their laptops. Pete stood beside them, waiting for his signal. "Can we get you something to drink?"

"Water would be great, thanks."

Dugan grabbed a bottle from the refrigerator, handed it to Rollins, then took a seat on the matching chair opposite him, pulling out a notebook.

Demaris studied the man for several minutes, then began, his voice gentle. "I know this has been such a stressful day for you, so I'll be brief. Can you recall when you first noticed that Wixie was gone?"

Rollins looked up with bloodshot, watery eyes. "Must've been about two, maybe a little later. She's in morning kindergarten. I picked her up about eleven-fifteen. Then we came home and had lunch. She's kind of given up her nap, but we—Palla and I—agreed that she should still have the routine of a quiet time. I read her a couple of stories, then closed the door and went down to my study. Then I realized I had to go to campus to pick up some documents, so I left Becca in the apartment watching TV"

"Do you have any idea why Wixie ran off?"

Rollins sat up straighter, his usual haughty demeanor suddenly in evidence. "What does this have to do with anything?"

"I'm not sure, but it's—"

"None of your goddamn business."

"Perhaps not, but I will ask and you will tell me, because we are trying to determine Wixie's whereabouts as well as her state of mind. We have no wish to pry into your personal affairs, but this is a murder investigation."

"Fine. You want to know just how shitty this day has been? Last night when I brought Wixie home—she's with me three days a week and every other weekend— she called Lily, my live-in girlfriend, a witch. Then Lily and I had a huge argument and she stalked out to stay with a friend. When I tried to talk with Wixie about it, she started whining to go back to her mother's. I finally got her to bed last night and off to school this morning, but as soon as she got in the car, she started up again about wanting to go home.

"As you observed, my relationship with her mother is not exactly cordial. Ever since we split up, Palla has done everything in her power to drive a wedge between Wixie and me. They live in the house I built, the only home Wix has ever known. I hate living in the dorm, but after giving Palla the house, I'm not exactly flush. Maybe next year I can afford to look for a small cottage, but even that won't be home to Wix."

"Prior to the witch comment, how did Wixie get along with your girlfriend?"

Rollins looked as though he might protest, but then he shook his head, leaning back, running long fingers through his shoulder-length hair. "Oil and water. And you can imagine what her mother thinks of her."

"Did you go out to look for her?"

"Not at first. Both the girls were gone, so I figured Wixie had gotten up and they'd taken a walk. Then Becca called, screaming about the woods, and I ran out to the fields."

"Is Wixie apt to go in the woods alone?"

"No, absolutely not. She loves the woods, but she's also afraid of them. Has never ventured near them without one of us. Then I ran into one of the grounds crew and they told me about Wixie. I went to the field, and the lacrosse players were just coming out. Becca was sitting on the ground, sobbing hysterically."

"Did she say anything?"

"No, just pointed to the path, so I thought she meant Wixie was in there. I went in pretty deep, way past where the woman was lying, calling Wixie's name."

"So you saw the body?" Demaris asked.

"Yes, but I didn't stop to gawk. My immediate concern was Wixie. I took the Weetamoe Loop that comes out near the head of school's house. I figured if she'd been in the woods at all, she would loop around and head to Palla's eventually. When I walk her home, sometimes we go that way, even if it's not as direct."

"I see. Did you see anyone?"

"I met a couple of village women jogging and told them to turn around and go back the way they're come."

"Oh?"

"It's a popular loop."

"Did you know them?"

"One was Sue LeBlanc. She works at Harbor Gym. Didn't recognize the other, but if I had to guess, it was probably someone from the gym. Since Sue's divorce, she practically lives there."

"Did you know the deceased, Gretchen Parker?"

He shook his head. "I've heard the name. Vicky, her daughter, teaches first grade at Wixie's school. We hope Wix'll be placed in her class next year. She's supposed to be great."

"Well, thank you, Mr. Rollins. We'll let you go. If you think of anything that might help in our investigation, please be in touch."

Pete handed him a card. "All our cell numbers are here."

Rollins nodded, shuffling toward the door. Hand on the knob, he turned back, gazing at Demaris. "I adore my daughter, Lieutenant. I believe you were divorced many years ago, so you know. It sucks."

CHAPTER 10

"Pete's steamed, boss," Greta said, pushing an unruly lock of hair from her face as she pulled up and parked at The Glen. Vicky Brown, Gretchen Parker's daughter, resided at the condominium complex by the creek, along with her roommate, Suzanna Costa, Pete, and his girlfriend, Hillary. The three women sometimes shared drinks by the pool on summer evenings and occasionally went to the gym together. Pete knew Vicky, but not well, so he thought it was perfectly appropriate for him to accompany his boss to talk with her. Demaris did not agree and set him to work with Stevens on computer research.

Demaris smiled over at her. "And this is unusual?"

She chuckled. "He probably won't speak to me all night."

"He'll get over it," Demaris said. "Come on."

As Greta knocked on the door, the scent of cumin and turmeric surrounded them. The delicious aromas appeared to be emanating from the apartment at the end of the hall. "Someone's making curry," she said as the door opened in front of them.

Vicky opened the door a crack, then wider once she recognized them. Eyes rimmed with tears, face a mask of red blotches, she appeared not to have changed when called away from school with the news of her mother. Her gray pencil skirt was stained with a green substance. Her white blouse, wrinkled and untucked, sported some of the same stains. Her dark hair stood up at odd angles as if she had been endeavoring to pull it out, and her black tights were torn at the knee.

"We're so sorry for your loss," he said quietly. "May we come in?"

She threw open the door and stood back.

"Is Suzanna here?"

She shook her head, sitting hard on the sofa. "Can't reach her. She's at a soccer game."

"Is there someone else we can call to come and be with you?"

"Suzanna will be home soon," she said. "And my aunt Lucy is on her way. She's hit traffic coming from Bell Harbor."

"Is she your mother's sister?"

Vicky nodded as her eyes darted around the room.

Greta followed her gaze for a minute, then asked, "Can I get you something? Water? Coffee? Tea?"

"I was looking for the Kleenex."

"Let me see what I can find," Greta said and disappeared down the hall in search of a bathroom.

Vicky stared at him, glassy-eyed. "Who would want to kill her? Everyone liked Mother."

"What has she been doing on this visit?"

"Seeing old friends, mostly. She's had lunches with some of the book club people, played a round of golf, went out to dinner last night."

"Was she having problems with anyone?"

"Not that I know of. I've been super busy with the start of school, so we've not spent much time together. We were supposed to go to have dinner with Aunt Lucy tonight."

This statement prompted a fresh spate of tears. Fortunately, Greta arrived at that moment and handed her a large box of tissues.

"I understand your mother was a widow?" he asked.

"Yes. Her third husband, Greg, died last year."

"What about the others?" Demaris said.

"My dad, her first husband, died of colon cancer at thirty-six."

"I'm sorry."

"I was four. I hardly remember him."

"What about her second husband?" he continued, as Greta took notes.

"Him I remember, Dennis Harrison. Only good thing about him was that he didn't stay around long. Mom married him the year after dad died. They were married for five years and in that time, I'd guess he had at least a dozen affairs. Broke Mom's heart and walked all over her. All he wanted was her money. My dad left her very well provided for, but if she'd stayed with Dennis, I'm sure she'd have been broke by now. He talked as if he had lots of money, but it was all smoke and mirrors. He spent everything he made and everything he could get his grubby little hands on. Mom finally screwed up the courage and gave him the boot."

"Did your mother keep in contact with Mr. Harrison?"

"I hope not. He's on wife number five, I think. They own a condo here in The Glen, but thank God they spend almost no time here. I think Mom told me Dennis lives somewhere in Florida."

Demaris looked at Greta and she nodded, making a note. "Are you an only child, then?"

"Yes."

"Did Mr. Harrison or her third husband have children?"

"Harrison had three by his first wife, but they weren't close, big surprise. There may be dozens of illegitimate kids running around. Greg had four children. They all live in Florida except his youngest daughter, Sarah, who's in graduate school in Chicago."

"Were you close to any of them?"

"Hardly knew them. Only met Sarah once and the others a few times. Never met Dennis's kids. They are older and, as I say, not close to their dad. On the rare occasions I stayed with Mom and Dennis, they were nowhere to be seen."

"It would be helpful to have the names and contact information for Mr. Parker's children and Mr. Harrison's, too, if you have them."

"Why?"

"You never know what someone might know or be able to contribute."

As he spoke, the door banged open and Suzanna Costa came in. "Oh, Vick, I am so so sorry," she said, flying across the room to embrace her friend.

Vicky collapsed, sobbing in her roommate's arms. As Suzanna patted her friend's back, making soft cooing sounds, she gazed up at them, eyes questioning.

Demaris and Burke stood. "Suzanna, at some point I or one of my detectives will want to speak to you, but for now we'll leave you two alone. I understand her aunt is on her way. Will you be okay?"

She nodded. Clearly they would not be okay, but there was nothing more to say. The detectives stepped into the hall and softly closed the door.

"Let's find out all we can about the step kids and Harrison."

"Yes, sir," she said, sliding into the driver's seat of her car.

"How's your mother?"

"'Bout the same. Dreading the winter. Can barely move her hands once the cold sets in."

"Who's with her today?"

"I've got one of her regular caregivers, Nancy. Hired her for the week, days and nights."

"Is that going to be too much for you?"

"No, sir. Mom loves Nancy. She'd rather spend time with her than me."

"I mean the extra expense."

"No, sir. Insurance pays for most of it, and my brother picks up the rest. He may be useless, but he's rich and has finally taken over most of her expenses."

"That's good."

"Yes, sir, thanks for asking."

CHAPTER 11

On her way home, Bess stopped at Village Market, a good-sized grocery store where most local residents shopped. Frip Daniels, the owner, had grown the store from a mom-and-pop operation to a destination market for local gourmands. People came to shop from many surrounding towns, and the market specialized in everything local from cheese, wine and catered foods to produce from the Old Harbor Friends school farm. Independently wealthy, Daniels kept prices low and competitive with chain stores and had built a vast, fiercely loyal client base. Rumor was that Village Market was also heavily subsidized by Harry Winthrop Senior, but the octogenarian always denied any involvement in the store when asked.

Rosemary Franklin was behind the register when Bess brought her basket through. "Hello, Ms. Dore, or should I say, Demaris?"

Bess smiled at the young woman. "It's Demaris."

"Congratulations! He's a major hunk and a huge catch. All the girls are jealous."

In her late twenties, Rosemary Franklin was what one might call an old soul. Her youthful hazel eyes danced with light as she contemplated Roger Demaris's hunkiness, but there was weariness in her posture. Her dark brown hair hung limp at her shoulders. Her complexion was pale, almost sallow. On the plump side, she was dressed in jeans and a man's oversized denim shirt, untucked, with a bright yellow Village Market apron tied loosely round her waist.

Bess laughed, loading her few things into the canvas bag she had brought. "I'll tell him that tonight. He'll be very flattered."

"How was your honeymoon?"

"Lovely, thanks. How're your parents?" Rosemary's stepmother, Margery Franklin, ran a small but successful gallery in Mattapoisett. Bob, Marge's husband and Rosemary's father, supplied most of the village's lobster. His boat consistently hauled the biggest catches, and he seemed to have the knack of setting his pots in the right places and knowing just when to pull them.

"Doing okay. You know Dad. He's out most of the time. Marge's doin' well at the gallery, I think. She's been devastated by poor Mrs. Parker's death."

"Yes, very tragic. Were you close to Gretchen Parker?"

"Not really. She was my stepmother's friend. Gretchen and Marge did stuff together mostly. Dad and Marge have only been together for a few years, four and a half dating and then three married, so Mrs. Parker had moved away by then. I think when she comes up, they have lunches and dinners."

"Did your dad know her?"

Rosemary paused and stared before replying. "Well, he knew who she was, like most everyone around here. But they didn't hang out or anything."

Bess suddenly noticed a line had formed behind her. "Oh, my, I've gotten you behind! Thanks so much, Rosemary. Say hi to Marge for me."

CHAPTER 12

After leaving Vicky Brown, Demaris directed Greta to head to the clinic to check in with Megan Krieger. When they arrived, Megan and her assistant were taking a short break for tea, seated in the anteroom just outside the lab. Both wore stained pink lab coats and their long, dark hair, Megan's curly, Bethany's straight, had been tied back in messy ponytails and stuffed under their puffy paper disposable lab hats. Megan was short, with freckles splayed over her turned-up nose. Her assistant was tall and slender with pale skin and delicate features. He had no idea where Megan would settle once her husband completed his residency, but he prayed that it would be nearby. She was bright and very competent, but she was also a decent, warm person, as was Bethany. It would be a shame to lose them.

He nodded and pulled up a chair. "Ladies, have you anything for us?"

"Time of death around nine this morning. Strangulation, by some kind of thin wire." Krieger rose and indicated that he should follow her. "See, the wire actually cut her skin in places."

They entered the cool, sterile lab and Demaris gazed down at Vicky Brown's mother. "Poor woman. Any signs of a struggle?"

"Don't think she knew what hit her. Someone spiked her morning coffee. She had enough diazepam in her system to fell an elephant. She might have been unconscious when he or she strangled her."

"That must've been a heavy load for the killer, draggin' her into the woods," Greta said.

"Wasn't too far, actually. Beyond the perimeter trampled by the lacrosse team, we found drag marks. They led to that small lot near the maintenance shed. It's only about twenty-five yards."

Greta looked from Megan to her boss. "Wouldn't she have noticed her morning coffee was spiked? Funny she didn't taste it."

"She was drinking one of those designer lattes, flavored with cinnamon and hazelnut and loaded with cream and sugar. That probably masked the taste."

"Any clues as to where she died?"

"Not really. We've pulled a few fibers from her shoes, and the bag she was in has some soil and grass samples, probably from the golf course, rubbed off the clubs. It's one of those golf club travel bags. Might want to check where they're sold locally and at the golf pro shops. You might get lucky, although everybody buys online now. Too bad the killer didn't leave his or her luggage tag on the bag."

"So the bag was used?"

"Yup. Ever smelled a ripe golf bag? Smells just like that one. Mix of mold, fresh cut grass, and eau de locker room."

"Prints?"

"Outside was wiped clean, sprayed with Windex, but we're about to pull the thing open and look at the inside. Killer might have gotten sloppy."

"So she was having a latte. Anything else?"

"Blueberry corn muffin, lots of butter."

"Greta?"

"I'm on it, boss. I'll phone Pete and ask them to check cafés, coffee shops, and area diners. Want us to go farther afield than Old Harbor?"

"Yup, Northport and Mattapoisett, at least. Check with Lois and Cathy, too. I'll wager that blueberry corn muffins are a staple on their breakfast menu. Someone could have ordered takeout."

"They do that? I *love* their muffins," Greta said, already planning tomorrow's breakfast.

"Any other trauma to the body? Find anything on her clothes?"

"Not much. Appears she was drugged, strangled, then dumped in the bag and carried to the woods. No unusual scraping on her shoes, which were Bella Doras., a local artisan brand of handmade shoes.," Megan said.

"Three hundred bucks minimum," Greta said.

Megan Krieger grinned. During a slow time, Burke had studied the fashion pages, learning a great deal about designer apparel for men and women. She also frequented the small shops and boutiques in the area whenever there was a lull in their investigations. Her research had been useful on several cases. "Good call. Bethany looked them up. Her clothes were Chico's brand, very popular with sixties set. Greta?"

"Modest cost. I'm guessing that ensemble cost about four hundred retail."

Bethany gave Burke a high five. "Good call, Gret!"

"That's about it, boss," Krieger said. "We've sent off tissue samples, and we may have a little more in a day or so."

"Thanks, Meg. Go home, both of you. I'll check in tomorrow."

*****

"Welcome home," Bess said, greeting him at the door. "You must be exhausted."

He drew her into his arms, the sensation of being home reaching every fiber of his being. "Not as tired as you. Look at this hallway. No boxes."

"You should see the kitchen. Hungry?"

"A little. Mostly hungry for you and our bed. Is it free of boxes?"

"It is. Come on. I have soup heating, and some nice bread, thanks to Lo and Cathy."

"Good friends," he murmured as he followed her into their simple but beautiful new kitchen. The cabinets were white, many glass-fronted, the counter a muted beige stone. The floor's wide pine boards, salvaged from an old farmhouse, gave the room a soft glow. Stunned to see the cabinets filled with glassware and china, he whistled. "You are a miracle worker, wife of mine."

She gave him a soft smile he liked to think of as his alone, and handed him a glass of Pinot Noir. "Had to do something to keep from worrying."

"I'm sorry, Bess. This was meant to be our time."

They sat beside each other on stools drawn up to the counter. Bess placed her hand over his. "We have plenty of time." Such a brave thing for her to say. Such an enormous leap of faith. She had already lost a husband and fiancé, the husband to cancer, the fiancé to murder. *Yes, a colossal leap of faith.*

He kissed her softly. "Yes, we do."

"Are you feeling better now, hunk of mine?"

"What?"

She laughed. "Saw Rosemary Franklin at the market today. She says you're a major hunk and a huge catch. All her friends are insanely jealous of me."

He chuckled, squeezing her hand. "Well, I've been called a lot of things in my day, but that's a new one. Cute kid. How's she doing? Always seems like a bit of a lost soul to me. Did she say anything about the Parker woman's death?"

"Only that her mom's devastated."

"They were good friends. Understandable. I imagine the book club is reeling. We'll head over to talk with Marge tomorrow."

By tacit agreement, they ceased discussing the case. Bess knew that Wixie Rollins was safely home, but the matter of Gretchen Parker's murder and the location of her body not twenty yards from where Harry Winthrop had been found a year ago was left for another day.

After their simple meal, they lay in each other's arms, gazing at the stars through the wall of windows opposite their bed. In daylight the windows offered extraordinary views of fields of wildflowers, bordered by stone walls that stretched to a blue line of ocean beyond.

"I am a lucky man," he whispered, kissing her softly.

"Me, too," Bess said, nestling closer, surprised to feel his arousal softly caressing her tummy. Smiling in the darkness, she moved closer, hand caressing him. "Why, husband of mine, are you sure you're not too tired?"

"Never," he said huskily. "I love you, Bess."

CHAPTER 13

Missing Bess ten minutes after kissing her good-bye, Demaris pushed open the Tavern door. His team sat at a window table, huge plates of breakfast in front of each. Tilly smiled as she paused with a tray full. "Children are fed. What can I get you?"

"Just coffee, thanks, Till. I ate at home."

"Your first breakfast in the new house, right?"

"Yup."

"You gonna be wearing that shit-eater grin every time the subject of the new Ms. Demaris comes up, aren't you?"

He laughed. "Probably."

"Good!"

Three pairs of eyes peered up from their food.

"Hey, boss," Pete said.

Greta groaned. "Oh, God, this is the best French toast I've ever eaten."

"That would be after two blueberry corn muffins," Pete said.

Greta's appetite was legendary. No matter what she consumed, she retained her thin, wiry frame. Demaris suspected that when she was at home, caring for her mother, she forgot to eat, so she made up for it when working on a case.

"Morning, Brendan. Your omelet good?"

Stevens nodded and smiled with a mouth full of food.

"Where are we?"

Reluctantly, Pete put down his fork and picked up his smartphone. "I checked in with Vicky Brown last night, then again on my way here this morning. She says she's doin' okay. Her roommate caught me outside their place and suggested we check into Derek Harper, some old boyfriend of Vicky's who didn't get along with the mom."

"I remember him," Stevens said. "He was a couple of years older than me, in my sister's class. Played basketball. Not great, but thought he was. Kind of a jerk."

Demaris looked from one to the other. "Do we know where Harper lives?"

Stevens eyed the basket of muffins, seeming to wonder if he could squeeze in one more. "Not in the village. Maybe Northport, sir. Want me to check?"

"Thanks, Brendan. Greta?"

"Stevens and I checked everywhere in town. Yesterday, the Café on Main, here, and the B and B all had blueberry corn muffins on the menu. This place buys them from the café, and Lois and Cathy make their own. Lois says no one bought any yesterday who wasn't staying there, and the few they served were to guests, no Gretchen Parker in sight. She did say that Garrett Rollins bought a bag of assorted muffins from her the day before."

"Did you ask Tilly and Rachel?"

"They both know Gretchen, and she did not eat here yesterday morning. In fact, they only served three muffins and gave the rest to the kitchen staff. As for the café, we spoke to Betty Sue Collins and she just rolled her eyes. You know what that place is like in the morning. Line for bakery stuff is out the door and down the street."

"Still, get their credit card receipts and check 'em, will you? What do we know about Gretchen Parker?"

Stevens and Greta grabbed their books. She spoke first. "Married three times. First husband, Vicky's dad died young. Then she married Dennis Harrison, who's been married, what, Brendan?"

"Five times, sir. Mrs. Parker was his second wife."

"Real scumbag, from what we've learned so far. Brendan has more about him in a sec. Victim's third husband, Greg Parker, was by all accounts a good guy. A widower. There may have been some resentment from his kids about the new wife. Has four, three sons and a daughter, all living in Florida around Naples, where Gretchen has lived the past few years. Want us to check into them?"

"Have they been notified?"

"Not yet," Pete said. "According to Vicky, they haven't been in contact since their father's death. He had money and left most of it to them."

Greta waited, watching her partner, until Dugan finished talking. "Gretchen Parker's sister, Lucy Cotter, lives in Bell Harbor. Sisters were close, but Gretchen and Bill Cotter, the husband, have never seen eye to eye. Sisters were planning to have dinner last night, right, Pete?"

Pete nodded.

"I'd like to talk to her," Demaris said. "She's coming up to be with Vicky. Greta, give them a call and ask when we could stop by, would you?" He sipped his coffee, staring out the window toward the woods. After several minutes, he turned to the junior officer. "So, Brendan, tell me about Mr. Harrison."

Stevens was still flipping pages in his notebook when the man himself burst through the Tavern door. "Speak of the devil," Stevens whispered.

Rachel met him at the entrance. "Good morning, Dennis. Breakfast for one, or will there be others joining you?"

"Where the hell are the cops investigating Gretchen's death?"

Not waiting for Rachel's answer, he gazed round the room until he spotted Demaris. "Who's in charge here?"

Dugan pushed back and started to stand. "Now look here, you."

Demaris waved him down and said calmly, "Mr. Harrison?"

"Who the hell are you?"

Buddha-like, Demaris gazed up at the sixty something man with a florid complexion, thinning salt-and-pepper hair, rheumy eyes. He had the build of a tennis player who carried about thirty extra pounds around his middle. "Mr. Harrison, if you wish to speak to me or any of my team, I will have my detectives escort you to our operations office in the guest house. If this is not a convenient time, we can arrange another. As you can see, most of us are finishing breakfast."

"What the hell are you talking about?"

"Pete?"

Dugan rose. "Come along, Mr. Harrison. You can take a seat at another table and wait, make an appointment for a later time, or come along with me to the guest house."

"Take your hands off me! I know you. You're that whippersnapper who dates the Dobbs girl, aren't you? Didn't I hear you left town and were working at some state job?"

"That would be the Regional Homicide Division and this is its head, my boss, Lieutenant Demaris."

"Okay, then, Lieutenant, it's you I want to speak to, not the second string."

Demaris took several deep breaths, nodded to Tilly, who had just refreshed his coffee, then stood. "Alright, Mr. Harrison, shall we? You two stay and finish your breakfasts," he said to Greta and Stevens. "Then, go back to your digging, okay?"

"Yes, sir," they said in unison.

CHAPTER 14

Harrison accompanied them out the back door, and the three strolled without a word until they were seated in the guesthouse, Harrison on the love seat, Demaris in a straight-backed chair. Pete sat beside Harrison in one of the easy chairs, note pad in hand.

"So, Mr. Harrison, how can we help you?"

"My wife's been murdered. I want to know where you are with the investigation."

"For what purpose?" Demaris asked.

"Because I care about Gretch."

"Ms. Parker is your ex-wife of some years, I believe?"

"What's your point, Lieutenant? I still loved her. We were very close."

"So, you've kept in touch?" Demaris said quietly.

"Of course."

"How?"

"Excuse me?" Harrison gave him a quizzical look.

"How have you kept in touch?"

"Email mostly. And we're both on Facebook."

"I see. Had you gotten together on this visit?"

"Didn't even know she was here."

"Isn't that surprising, given your closeness?"

"No, I wasn't her keeper. She might not have even known I was in town."

"Why were you in town? I understand you live in Florida now?"

"We maintain a residence here."

"We?"

"My wife Carla and I."

"Ah, yes, Ms. Whitmarsh. She is your fifth wife, I believe?"

"Yes, I've been married five times. Carla's it, though. I've found the one."

"Is she with you this trip?"

"Yes, but she's in Wellesley right now visiting her sister. Once she returns, we'll head home to Naples."

"And, where is this residence you maintain?"

"The Glen. We have a corner unit. Rarely use it, but I hate hotels. Prefer to have my own space when I'm up here."

"How often is that?"

"Couple of times a year. One of my kids lives up the coast. Another's in Boston and one teaches at Greenleaf."

"So you don't stay with them when you're in town?"

"No, we're not exactly close."

"Yet you come up to see them?"

"Carla's got family around here, too. My kids and I have a dinner, catch up. That's it."

Demaris recognized that he was way off course, but decided to follow the threads of Harrison's life a bit farther. "Who is the mother of your children, if you don't mind my asking?"

"Not that it's any of your business, but they're all products of my first marriage. Their mother, Angelina, passed away some years ago."

"Suicide, I believe?"

"Yes."

"Your children must have been quite young. Did you become both mother and father to them?"

"Not exactly. Angelina had full custody, and her will specified that her brother and his wife would raise the kids."

"Isn't that a bit unusual with a parent living?"

"Believe it or not, I was a bit of an asshole in those days. Too much partying, way too much drinking. When we divorced, the settlement agreement specified this guardianship arrangement, and I signed off on it for two reasons. One, I didn't have to give Angelina the millions she was demanding. Two, frankly, I didn't want to be saddled with three little kids. My brother-in-law's filthy rich. His wife, Mindy, was a terrific mother to my kids. Steele and Mindy never had kids of their own, so they were thrilled to have them. Seemed like the best thing for everyone. They gave my three a wonderful home. Certainly a better home than I could have provided."

"And your brother-in-law, do he and his wife still live locally?"

"Mindy died. He's remarried. Steele and Claire Rubin live in Mattapoisett, same house where the kids grew up."

"Your brother-in-law is Steele Rubin?"

"The very same. Do you know him? Bit of a snob. Has a stick up his ass, but he was good to my kids. Sent 'em all to private schools from kindergarten on. Paid for college, too."

Demaris thought back to an earlier case in which he had spent some time with Claire Rubin, leader of a local women's book club. He knew Claire from around town as she and her late husband, Dickie, had lived in Northport. Their daughter, Ellen, had attended school with him until she enrolled at Old Harbor Friends as a ninth grader. He could not picture Steele Rubin, but then, Mattapoisett was a community unto itself.

"So, Mr. Harrison, let me recap. You and your wife maintain a condominium in the village that you use a few times a year to visit with family. You're only here for a few days, hadn't seen or heard from Gretchen Parker, and weren't planning to see her on this trip. So perhaps you could enlighten us as to the reason for this trip north and where you were yesterday morning between seven and noon."

"As I told you, my wife is visiting family."

"Then why come here? Why not just stay in Wellesley?"

"My sister-in-law and I do not get along. While Carla was up there, I could visit with old friends around here and try to rally my kids for a meal."

"And have you?"

"Rallied them? Not yet."

"How about old friends? Have you seen any this trip?"

"Not yet."

"But you're leaving anyway?"

"If you must know, I'm hoping to see one son and my daughter tonight. I may have lunch with my other son tomorrow, then catch up with some old tennis buddies ."

"Where were you yesterday morning?"

"At the condo, sleeping, reading papers. Had a late breakfast at the café. Ask Betty Sue or Frank. We had a great time catching up."

"What time was that?"

"Around ten-thirty, maybe eleven."

"And do you play golf?"

Harrison stared at him, perplexed by the abrupt shift in topic. "Excuse me?"

"Golf? Are you a golfer?"

"Yes, but I prefer tennis."

"Did you bring your clubs on this trip?"

"Why? Is that how Gretch died? Someone hit her with a golf club?"

Ignoring Harrison's question, Demaris reiterated, "What about your clubs, Mr. Harrison? Are they with you on this trip?"

"I keep an old set here. Prefer courses in Naples, but occasionally someone wants to play and I drag them out."

"Where are they stored?"

"In the condo's storage unit. Why?"

"Are they packed in anything?"

"Excuse me?"

"Are they open, just standing in the storage unit?"

"I'm not even sure. It's been over a year since I used them. Seldom go in the storage unit. I think they were in an old golf travel bag last time I looked."

"What color is the bag?"

"Excuse me?"

"The travel bag, what color is it?"

"Black, I think. I honestly can't remember."

"Might I send one of my detectives out to take a look?"

"What's this about, anyway?"

"Ms. Parker's body was found zipped in a golf travel bag."

"Jesus Christ! Well, it sure as hell wasn't mine!"

"So you won't mind if we take a look?"

"Sure, knock yourself out."

"That's all for now, Mr. Harrison. Detective Dugan will follow you home and have a quick peek in the storage closet, if that's convenient?"

Harrison shrugged and stood up, meekly following Pete out the door.

Demaris leaned back and ran his fingers through his hair. What kind of a tangled, gnarly mess had they stepped into here?

CHAPTER 15

Lucy Cotter told Greta she preferred to come to the guest house. She appeared less than half an hour after the call. A pleasant-looking woman dressed in khaki slacks and a gold crew neck sweater, she appeared to be around sixty. Her salt-and-pepper hair was cut short. She wore no makeup, and her eyes were red and puffy. She carried an enormous red purse slung over her shoulder, which somehow did not match the rest of her.

"Hello, Ms. Cotter. Come in," Demaris said. "Thanks for responding so quickly. We are deeply sorry for your loss."

"Thank you," she said, dabbing her eyes with a shredded tissue.

"Can we get you something to drink?"

"No, thanks. I can only stay a minute. I don't want to leave Vicky alone, and there are so many arrangements to be made with the funeral home and the service."

"Of course. I promise we'll be brief."

They sat on opposite sides of the table. He cleared off the files and papers in the space separating them. "I understand that you were meant to have dinner with your sister tonight?"

"Yes, I was coming up. Bill, my husband, and Gretchen don't get along. It's easier that way."

"So you hadn't seen her yet on this visit?"

"No, we had spoken on the phone several times."

"How did she seem?"

"Up and down, I'd say. The first time, the day she arrived, she sounded herself. Really upbeat, looking forward to seeing friends. Did you know her?"

"Only slightly, from school functions."

"Gretch was a warm, outgoing person. Loved everyone, especially Vicky. She was such a kind, generous friend, parent, and sister. She's my only sibling, Lieutenant. What will I do without her?"

He waited several minutes to allow a fresh spate of tears to let up. "Can you think of anyone who might wish her harm?"

"No, no one."

"Were you friendly with her husbands?"

"Roger, Vicky's dad, was a love, but I never warmed to Greg Parker. Barely knew the man, as they were living in Florida most of the time. We sisters would usually get together mostly without our husbands when she came up."

"Have your husband and Gretchen never been close?"

She paused and stared at him before responding. "They are very different personalities. I love Bill, but he's extremely shy, almost antisocial. He's a writer. Writes ad copy for small businesses. If he can avoid it, he almost never leaves the house. My sister was the polar opposite. Even so, they were okay until she married Dennis, whom we pretend was never a part of our family."

"Oh. Was there a particular issue?"

"Bill strongly advised Gretchen not to marry Dennis. He grew up in Northport and knew him. More importantly, some of the businesses he writes for knew Dennis."

"Had they had problems with Mr. Harrison?"

"He's not the most trustworthy person. Anyone who's been in partnership with him gets burned in some way or other, personally and professionally. Bill urged her to walk away from Dennis, but she was infatuated with Mr. Charming, so she ignored him. They've barely spoken since. He thinks my sister is frivolous, and I'm not going to change his mind. Despite all that, he's devastated about her death, just as I am."

"You alluded to a change in your sister from your phone conversations this past week?"

"Oh, yes, sorry. The first call, she was happy and upbeat, but the last time we spoke, the night before she died, she was distraught and said she had had some very distressing news."

"But she didn't say what?"

"No, said she'd tell me tonight. Said she needed my advice as to how to proceed."

"And that was the last time you spoke to her?"

"Yes," she said softly, reaching for the tissue box at the far end of the table.

"Thank you, Ms. Cotter. We'll let you go. Do you suppose if I sent two of my team members down to your home, Mr. Cotter would speak with them? I'd like to know a little more about his understanding of Mr. Harrison's business practices."

"I'm sure he would. He's happy as a clam to have people visit. Just don't ask him to come to you. Unless Vicky needs me, I'll head home tonight and be back and forth all week, but feel free to call Bill anytime."

'Thank you. Can one of my detectives drive you home?"

"No, thanks, my car's right outside. Off to the funeral home now. Is it likely Gretchen's body will be released soon?"

"Probably not for a few days."

"Well, then, we'll plan the memorial anyway."

*****

Demaris asked Greta to phone Bill Cotter to see if she and Stevens might pop down to talk with him between their computer work and their research into the whereabouts of Harrison's children.

"Sure thing, boss." She grabbed her cell and the sheet with the Cotters' home phone number.

As Greta stepped into the bedroom, he phoned the Rubins. Claire answered, and they agreed on a five o'clock meeting in Mattapoisett.

"Cotter said the best time would be around three," Greta said, resuming her seat at the counter and opening her laptop.

"Good. Thanks, Greta."

As she and Stevens began pecking away at their computers, he dialed Bess's cell and stepped outside. "Hello, my love. How are you doing?"

"Roger, what a nice surprise. I'm actually at school, meeting with students. Can I call you back?"

"No need. Just wanted to hear your voice. See you tonight. Love you."

"Me, too."

CHAPTER 16

As he clicked off from Bess, Demaris spied Pete's car pulling in behind the guest house. "Any luck?"

"The golf bag is gone. Harrison claims he hasn't seen it in over a year."

"Is his storage unit locked?"

"Nope, but it's filled with a bunch of junk no one in their right mind would want."

They headed into the guest house, and Pete grabbed a water from the fridge. "Anyone else want something?"

They all shook their heads as Demaris said, "I'll have one of Meg's team bring the bag down. Call Harrison and let him know to stay put this afternoon, or at least let us know his whereabouts."

"Will do."

"After that, let's you and me head over to the school. I'd like to talk with Pru Marsden and see if she has any knowledge of Gretchen Parker and this whole mess."

"Sure thing, Rodge." Pete was the only person allowed to call him Rodge. "Are you thinking there's a connection between Wixie running away and Gretchen Parker's murder?"

"No, but this case has tendrils everywhere. It'll take us weeks just to track down all Dennis Harrison's former lovers. Somehow, I think he's connected to this."

"What's the deal with him anyway? How does an ugly ol' lech like him have women swooning all over him?"

Greta looked up from her computer. "There's something about him, kind of a magnetism. Didn't you feel it when he was here?"

"The hell I did not!" Pete said, face red with indignation.

"Well, I bet if we ask Hill, she'll say she knows what I'm talking about. Surely she's seen darling Dennis around the condo pool."

"Never said a thing to me."

Greta waved her arms. "I rest my case."

"Alright, you two," Demaris said. "Enough. We've got work to do."

Stevens cleared his throat, and his boss gazed at him over his reading glasses.

"Brendan, have you something to contribute to this discussion?"

"Well, sir, I mean, yes sir." He glanced at his idol, who was now glaring in his direction. "I sort of get what Greta's saying. There's something about his eyes, you know. They're sort of hypnotic."

Greta clapped her hands. "That's it, that's the word I was looking for—hypnotic! Thank you, Brendan, hypnotic, yes. There's also the way he invades your personal space. No boundaries…he just walks right in."

Pete threw up his hands. "Oh, for Christ's sake, has everyone around here lost their mind?"

"Walks right in," Demaris said. "Interesting way to put it. There's been quite a lot of that in this case."

"You don't agree with them, do you, Rodge?"

Demaris chuckled. "No accounting for taste in matters of the heart, but enough about Dennis Harrison for now. Let's go see the headmistress, shall we? And Greta and Brendan, I want a list of every woman who's ever batted an eyelash at Dennis Harrison, or who has been foolish enough to fall under his charms. Comprende?"

Greta pushed back in her chair, blowing a lock of hair from her eyes. "How far back?"

"Far as you can. Man's left destruction and broken hearts everywhere, and I want to know everyone whose life has been ruined by the hypnotic Mr. Harrison."

As Pete rolled his eyes and opened the door, Clarice Wills stepped in. "Hello, Roger, Pete. You look like you're on your way out. Have you got a minute?"

Surprised to see the bookseller, Demaris stepped back. "Of course. Come in, Clary."

"I won't stay long. I left a *be back soon* sign on the shop door."

"Here, sit. Want something? We have water, juices, soda?"

"No, thanks."

He took a seat on the love seat beside her, waiting.

His friend looked tired, dark circles under her violet eyes. Her long curly hair hung limp, the auburn streaked with gray. A diminutive woman who called herself the last hippie in town, Clarice usually wore peasant blouses, floral skirts, and Birkenstock sandals. The sandals, often augmented with socks, were replaced by Uggs when the cold weather set in. True to form today, she wore a lacy off-white blouse, its cuffs frayed and gray. A thin knitted shawl was draped round her shoulders, and her wide, dark purple skirt almost reached her ankles.

"Haven't seen you lately," she said.

"No, our cases have been mostly up north."

"Until now."

"Yes."

"Then there was your honeymoon. Congratulations on your marriage."

"Thank you. How have you been?"

"Been better, honestly. Teenage daughters are not easy on their mothers. It's been a rough year with Becca."

"I'm sorry to hear that. Are you here about her?"

"Sort of. Not really. I don't know, actually. I just wanted to talk to you so your picture of Becca was a bit fuller than Palla's."

"You know me better than that. I've known Becca since she was a baby."

"Yes, but she almost grown now."

"Yes."

"Palla hates her and hates me. She'd say anything."

"Are you under the impression that Becca's in trouble?"

"One of your officers called Garrett's this morning and said you wanted to speak with her. Becca was hysterical. Her father was at school, so she called me. Do you need to question her?"

"Yes, but only to fill in a few of the holes in Wixie's running away episode. We wondered if Becca might have been with her initially, then become distracted. I wondered if she might have seen anything or anyone. Is she with you today? I could come myself and talk with her."

"She's staying with Garrett. She's not happy with me because I impose a curfew and other rules, and she claims she's an adult and can do what she wants."

"Is she at her father's today?"

"I'm not sure, but you could call her cell. Please, Roger, could you do it? She knows you and would feel more comfortable if you talked with her instead of a stranger."

"Of course."

"She's a good girl. She's lost her way at present, but she's going to find it again."

"I'm sure she will."

"Thank you. Here's the number." She scribbled on a Post-it note and handed the paper to him. "I'll let you get on with things."

"Good to see you. I'll stop in for a cup of tea soon."

"I hope so." Lovely, sad eyes stared at him, and Demaris could see she was on the verge of tears.

"Can Officer Stevens walk you back?"

"Absolutely not. I'm fine. See you soon."
Clarice Wills departed, leaving them staring at the door.

CHAPTER 17

They found Becca Rollins in a lawn chair in the grassy stretch behind the dorm where her father lived. She was reading Mann's *The Magic Mountain*, bespectacled eyes riveted to the page.

"Becca?" he said softly, hoping not to startle her.

She gazed up at them over her glasses.

"How have you been?"

She shrugged and dropped the book on the ground. Dressed in torn blue jeans and a faded Old Harbor Friends sweatshirt, she looked younger than her eighteen years. She had her mother's delicate features but her father's dark coloring and intense, angry eyes.

"You might be able to guess why we're here?" Pete grabbed two lawn chairs and set them near her. Demaris pulled his directly in front of her.

"Wixie." She spit out the name. "These days everything's about Wixie."

"Can you tell us about yesterday?" Demaris said, voice soft.

"As usual, the spoiled brat was whining and fussing. Dad dumps her on me every other minute."

"Was he home, then?"

"No, he put her in her room for rest time. What a joke! Then he said he had something important to do on campus. Bullshit, of course. Just wanted a break from the constant whining."

"So, can you tell us what happened?"

"She was crying to go home. She doesn't think of the dorm as home. Home is only where Mommy is. I told her she'd have to wait until my dad got home, but she screamed and slammed the door to her room. I was in the kitchen when I spied her with her backpack, sneaking out the door. I let her go, then followed her."

"For how long?"

"The whole time. I didn't want her to see me so I hung back. I was shocked that she dared go into the woods by herself. I followed her down the path, but lost sight of her for a minute. Pretty soon, I saw her racing back toward me and I ducked behind a tree. That was when I saw the guy with the mask and I freaked. He had started to follow Wixie, but stopped when he saw her running toward the lacrosse players."

"Did you get a good look at him?"

"Not really. I was crouched down, hiding first from her, then him. When I looked up, he was gone."

"Anything? Hair color? Shoes? Pants?"

"Black jeans and black running shoes. Couldn't see his hair. He had a Spiderman hood over his whole head."

"So, he passed by where you were hiding?"

"Yes. I didn't dare move, but I saw his feet."

"Height? Anything about his build?"

"Maybe as tall as my dad? Kind of average build, I guess. I didn't really see."

"Did the stranger speak?"

"Nope."

"So, what happened next?"

"I listened till I knew he had gone back up the path. Then I got up and ran out of there as fast as I could. By the time I got to the field, Wixie was gone."

"Thanks, Becca. We'll let you get back to Thomas Mann. Do you like him?"

"We had to read *Death in Venice* last year for AP English and I liked it, so thought I'd try this one."

He nodded. "I was always partial to *Doctor Faustus*. Take care."

Pete returned the chairs to their original places and the two men headed off. "*Magic Mountain*? Is that about an amusement park?"

Demaris chuckled but said nothing. Dugan knew the book, or at least something about the author. Of that he was certain. As they neared the car, his cell phone rang. Greta.

"What'cha got?"

"They just dropped off the golf bag."

"Good, call Dennis Harrison and ask him to stop by the guest house. If he refuses, have Stevens pick him up. You stay there with the bag."

CHAPTER 18

Tall, with ramrod-straight posture, Pru Marsden appeared to be in her fifties. Her hair was almost snow white, her angular, handsome face unlined, her deep blue eyes serious but warm. She was dressed in brown tweed slacks and a beige cardigan, a string of pearls round her neck her only adornment. "So good to finally meet you, Lieutenant. Your reputation precedes you." She reached out and gave him a firm handshake.

"Uh-oh, so you've already had an earful."

"All good, I assure you. You have the respect of many in this community. Please sit. You, too, detective."

The headmistress's office was a study in Quaker simplicity with its stark white walls and sparse furnishings. Painted bookshelves held an assortment of books interspersed with artifacts one might associate with a world traveler—wooden tribal masks, delicately carved birds, silk paintings, stone carvings, and many framed photographs. As Demaris took the seat she offered, he glimpsed a photo of the lady herself, standing in front of what appeared to be China's Great Wall. Pete shook her hand, then stepped back to sit in a matching chair, silently taking notes.

"You are well traveled, Ms. Marsden," Demaris said, eyes traveling round the room.

"My husband, Philip, loves to travel. He plans the trips, and I gladly accompany him when my school schedule allows. He's retired, a bit older than me."

"Do you have children?"

"Mine are grown and live far away. One in the southwest, the other overseas. Philip's children do not live close by, either, except for his daughter in Boston."

"So, how are you finding Old Harbor, the school and village?"

"I love it. Fits me at this time in my life. I feel like I'm only just getting my feet on the ground after last year and my family situation."

"I'm sorry. Your mother, wasn't it?"

"Yes, she lived a long, wonderful life. I was very grateful to spend time with her at the end."

"Yes."

"I don't mean to sound rude, Lieutenant, but I fear my secretary may call me away for some crisis or another if we talk for too long. I'm assuming this is not a social call?"

"No, sorry. We're here about Gretchen Parker, the woman who was found in the woods near campus."

"Yes, very tragic about Ms. Parker. This village and those woods have seen too much violence the past few years. It is very hard on everyone."

"Did you know her?"

"I've met her once or twice at fund raisers. She was an Old Harbor Friends graduate. Did you know that?"

"No. I'm surprised she didn't send Vicky, her daughter, to the school."

"I believe Vicky's father was very adamant that she attend public schools. When he died, Gretchen acceded to his wishes and kept Vicky in the public system. She has been a generous donor to OHF, though. Very loyal, keeps in touch. She and her third husband, Greg Parker, used to host alumni gatherings in Naples and a yearly cocktail party here. They were enthusiastic supporters of the school."

"Did Mr. Parker have any affiliation with the school?"

"No, I don't think so. He did it for her. He seemed quite devoted to his wife."

"Have you ever met Mr. Parker's children?"

"No, to my recollection they have never been to Old Harbor, but as a newcomer, I am not the best person to ask. Perhaps Peter Thurbert, the previous head, or maybe Todd Bridgham, our Upper School head, might know."

"Can you think of anyone at the school who might have had an issue with Gretchen Parker?"

"No, I'm sorry. Aside from their yearly cocktail parties and a visit now and then to see her daughter, I don't believe they spent much time in the village."

"Well, thank you for your time, Ms. Marsden. I'm sure you are very busy."

"Pru, please. Of course, always happy to help, and am so glad to finally meet you. Can I walk you out?"

"No need. We know the way. Good-bye."

*****

Demaris checked his phone and spied a text from Greta. *Harrison coming at one.* As they made their way to the car, they waved at Bess' dear friend and colleague, Jane Fellows, the upper school biology teacher.

"Some honeymoon," she called before disappearing into the Commons, the student center.

He shrugged and smiled.

"Wanta stop in and say hi?" Pete asked, speaking for the first time since he had greeted Pru Marsden. It was one of the qualities Demaris most appreciated about his assistant, his comfort with silence when they were working.

"Thanks, but she's busy. Will try to get home early tonight." Home had taken on a whole new meaning for him. "You hungry?"

"Always."

"Call Greta and ask her to order lunch from Tilly. Chicken salad wrap for me."

CHAPTER 19

Over lunch, the team planned their afternoon. Demaris and Pete were due to talk with Claire and Steele Rubin, and Stevens and Greta planned to pay a visit to Bill Cotter, then try and find Derek Harper, whom they had learned lived in Derryport, a short ride up the coast. Then, they would return and continue to research anyone connected with Gretchen Parker. "I can't believe Harrison's not in it up to his eyeballs," Pete said as the man himself knocked at the door.

"Come in, Mr. Harrison," Demaris called. Greta moved to open the door.

Harrison looked from one to the other of them before his eyes rested on the golf bag lying on the floor. "May I?" he asked, bending over to have a closer look.

"Yes, please." Demaris rose and came to stoop beside him.

"Can I turn it over?"

"Yes, of course."

"Yup, it's mine. See this tear?" He held up one end. "Airline did this the last time I used it. And this is my handwriting, see here? The tag's been ripped off, but you can just see the last two numbers of my zip code in Naples. Was poor Gretchen in this when you found her?"

Demaris nodded. "Can you be as precise as possible about the last time you remember seeing the bag?"

"Well, it would have to have been a year ago July. Didn't use it at all this past summer."

"So you put it in your storage closet and haven't looked in there for over a year?"

"No, that's the last time I used the bag. I was in and out of the closet all this summer. I'm pretty sure the bag was there." He closed his eyes. "Lemme think. We brought out the patio chairs, and I'm pretty sure it was there then, 'cause I did some rearranging. Then I came up in August, a few weeks back. When I put the patio furniture away, I moved things around and, yup, it was there, 'cause I actually looked it over thinking I might take it to Goodwill. In fact, now that I think of it, I put the bag and a bunch of stuff in a box right near the door, intending to take it to Goodwill on my next visit."

"And did you?"

"No, box is still there. I was planning to do that tomorrow, before I went back to Naples."

"I'd like you to go through the box, see if it contains the items you remember. I'll have Officer Stevens accompany you back. After you've checked it, we'll borrow it, if you don't mind."

"Be my guest. You can take it to Goodwill just as easily as I can. We're thinking of selling the Glen condo soon and want to start clearing things out."

"And the storage closet was locked?"

"Not since last year. I lost the key and had to break the lock. Haven't gotten around to replacing it. Nothing much of value in there. To my knowledge, thefts are rare or nonexistent at The Glen."

"I don't suppose you can think of anyone who might want to harm Ms. Parker?"

"No, everyone loved her. How's dear Vicky doing? She must be devastated."

"Yes."

"And that roommate of hers, Suzie?"

"Suzanna Costa?"

"Yes, she was like a daughter to Gretch. Very close. Can't remember the girl's background, but I don't think her family was worth much. Gretch was very good to her."

Demaris motioned to Stevens, who stood and moved to the door. "Well, thank you, Mr. Harrison."

CHAPTER 20

"Okay, you two," Demaris said as he joined Greta and Brendan at the farmhouse table. Pete had gone over to get four Tilly's teas, and Demaris wanted to debrief before they headed off in separate directions. "Okay, I want to hear everything you've dredged up on Harrison, his wives, his kids, whatever. And Greta, what have you found out so far about the Rubins?"

Greta pushed back from her laptop and grabbed her notebook. "Yes, sir. They've been married five years. Second marriage for both. As you know, Claire's first husband was Dickie Myers."

"Yes, he was a great guy. Died too young," Demaris said.

Greta continued. "Dickie's sister, Lee, lives here in the village, in a cottage near campus. She's one of the book club ladies."

"Yes, I remember her from the Winthrop case," Demaris said. It helped ease the horror and sadness to call it "the Winthrop case" rather than the murder of his wife's beloved fiancé.

The door opened, and Pete appeared carrying a tray with a plate of cookies and a pitcher of tea. Stevens hopped up and took four glasses from the kitchen cupboard.

Greta glanced up at him, then continued. "Lee's had a troubled life. No kids. Ex-husband an abusive, alcoholic asshole. He's a shell fisherman, lives in Northport. They were close to Claire's kids growing up."

"I remember him, Jack Farraday."

"Yes. Lee's a travel writer and had pretty good success until the Internet made printed travel guides almost obsolete. She's traveled the world. Still writes a monthly online travel column. The only reason I'm elaborating on her is that rumor has it she had a fling with Dennis Harrison."

"Like every woman within fifty miles," Dugan said, setting down the tray.

"Where'd you hear that?" Demaris asked.

"Suzanna Costa told us when Pete and I interviewed her. Subject only came up because she was bad-mouthing Harrison, as most people do, and spontaneously began listing some of his conquests."

"I'd like to hear that list, but let's stick to the Rubins right now."

"Okay, they've been together five years. Claire has three grown kids, whom I believe you know? Ellen is your age, forty-three, and from our check of her school records, she was in your class at Northport, right?"

"Just through middle school. Then she came to Old Harbor Friends. Her brother, too."

"Ellen is a realtor in Northport, married, two kids. Dickie Junior is forty-five, married, three kids, works for an investment firm in Providence, and lives in Barrrington, Rhode Island. Hollis is forty-four and a golf pro at the Mattapoisett Eagle's Nest course. He's unmarried and lives with Claire, and now Claire and Steele during the summer months. Has a job as a pro somewhere in Florida during the winter. Want me to find out where?"

Demaris shook his head. "We can ask Claire when we see her, if it seems relevant."

"As you know, Steele raised the three Harrison kids, but I'll let Brendan tell you. He's the one who's been digging up their info."

Stevens set down his tea and sat up straight.

"Yes, sir. Mr. Rubin is a bit older than his wife. She's sixty-five. He's seventy three. A venture capitalist, he still works. Office is in Providence, but he mostly works from home and does a bit of traveling back and forth to New York. His first wife, Mindy, was killed in a boating accident seven years ago. Everyone loved her. Claire Myers was one of her good friends, and I guess they, Ms. Myers and Mr. Rubin, got together after. The first Mrs. Rubin and her husband basically raised Harrison's three kids, who were young when their mom, Angelina, died. Angelina was Steele's sister, and she had full custody of them. Her will specified that her brother would raise them."

"Yes, Mr. Harrison told us about that rather unconventional arrangement."

"From all I've been able to learn, he wasn't a suitable parent for three young children. Dennis Junior, Lena, and Steele are all in their forties now. Went to grade school in Mattapoisett, then Moses Brown in Providence. They all graduated from there and went to good colleges, all paid for by Mr. Rubin. Dennis Junior went to Brown and is a history professor at Greenleaf. He and his wife, Ruth, are parents of three, two girls and a boy.

"Their eldest, Maisie, was born out of wedlock when Dennis and Ruth were high school seniors."

"I'd like to know more about that," Demaris said quietly.

"Yes, sir, we'll keep digging. Anyway, Lena went to Rhode Island School of Design and majored in fashion design. She's married, lives in Sharon and owns a designer dress shop on Newbery Street in Boston, no kids. Steele is the youngest at forty-one. He went to Bowdoin and runs a landscaping business in Sage Harbor. His wife, Lizzy, is a French teacher at Old Harbor Friends and they live in the village, in the old Macomber place. They bought it two years ago and gutted it, and now it's supposed to be a showplace."

Demaris leaned back in his chair, running fingers through his hair. "Very thorough. Thanks, both of you. Don't s'pose in any of that you found someone with a reason to kill Gretchen Parker?"

"Not yet," she replied, "But I don't think it's Derek Harper. Brendan and I went to Derryport and found him after work. Nice guy, hadn't seen much of Vicky, but recently they've had a couple of dinners. He described them as friends, nothing more. When we mentioned Gretchen Parker's death, he looked genuinely distraught, more for Vicky than for any great love for the mother."

"Any other thoughts?"

"Not really, but Angelina's kids and her brother hated anyone who might have come between her and Dennis, so I don't imagine they loved Gretchen since she ended up marrying the louse."

"But she didn't break them up?"

"No," Greta said. "Dennis was involved with Lee and probably three or four others before he wooed Gretchen. I suppose she was the most visible, since they did marry. Angelina's suicide was only two months after that wedding."

"Yeah," Pete said, sitting beside Stevens, waving a half-eaten chocolate cookie. "Suzanna Costa went on and on about how much they hated Parker, didn't she?"

Greta nodded. "No love lost there."

"Okay, I'll read through your notes on the Costa interview later. Who else was on the Harrison conquest list she provided?"

"Wanda Borden, a waitress at Eagle's Nest, Lee Myers, and Marge Franklin. Remember her? She was one of the book club ladies. In her late fifties. Owns a small gallery in Mattapoisett."

He nodded. "Yes, she hangs many of Palla Forest's paintings."

"She's pretty successful. Franklin, I mean. She makes a good bit on Forest's work as well as the other artists she hangs. Franklin herself does local landscapes that also sell well. Summer people pay big bucks for them. Her husband's a lobsterman, a little younger than Margery, who, as you probably remember, is a jogger and yoga teacher and looks much younger than she is."

"Anyone else?"

"Well, there are Harrison's other wives. We're just digging into them now, but both live in Florida. Then there's his current wife, Carla. Again, we're just getting started."

"Okay, well keep at it. Pete, time for us to roll. Tomorrow we need to talk to Lee Myers, Marge, Wanda, and whomever else you dredge up. I'd like to talk to Palla Forest, too."

"Why, boss?" she asked, handing him the notebook containing the Costa interview.

"Just a hunch. Take care, you two. After Pete and I finish up in Mattapoisett, I'm heading home. You do the same. We'll start up early tomorrow."

CHAPTER 22

Number eighteen Beachcomber Terrace lived up to its name. It was literally on the beach, with only a slight rise separating the sweeping lawn from the sand.

"Wouldn't want to be here in a hurricane," Pete said, pulling up beside a Volvo SUV parked in the shell-covered drive. An enormous shingled mansion stretched out before them, all turrets, chimneys, towers, and porches.

"That's why they built the barriers," Demaris said, pointing southward to the enormous seawalls that blocked this part of the coastline from the direct ocean.

"Kind of an odd place for seawalls, isn't it?"

"It's amazing what money and influence will get you these days. This is a far cry from Claire and Dickie's colonial in Northport. Growing up, I thought their house was a mansion, but compared to this, it was a shack."

"So she's come up in the world, then?"

"Maybe. Let's go."

Claire Rubin answered their knock and ushered them into a large conservatory at the back of the house. Windows on three sides provided unobstructed views of the Atlantic Ocean, which looked as if it might lap at the foundation at high tide. The green expanse of lawn was uninterrupted except when one looked north, where there was an enormous wooden play set with a house, swings, and slides. Gazing at it, Demaris said, "Grandchildren, I'm guessing?"

"Yes. Don't mention it when Steele arrives. He hates it. Once his children were grown, he had all the jungle gyms and swings ripped out and the lawn redone, but I wanted my grandchildren to have fun and want to come to stay."

"The Atlantic isn't fun enough?" Demaris asked, smiling warmly.

"You sound just like my husband, but we can't swim twelve months of the year. Besides, his grandchildren love the play set, too. Please sit. Steele got delayed in town but just called. He's on his way and will be here soon. Can I get you something to drink?" She waved to a table where pitchers of water and iced tea and an assortment of wines and soft drinks sat alongside an ice bucket and an array of glassware. It was clear she had prepared carefully for their visit.

"Water would be great. Pete?"

"Water for me, too, thanks." His assistant took a seat to his right. Their hostess poured the waters and a glass of white wine for herself, to which she added several ice cubes. Claire Rubin was tall and thin with patrician features and shoulder-length salt-and-pepper hair held back with a thin velvet band. She wore khaki slacks and a sky-blue tailored blouse that turned her green eyes to silky blue. Her belt was slim, buttery leather with a silver and turquoise buckle.

"Ah, I hear Steele now," she said, handing them their drinks, then turning to pour a very large goblet of red wine. "Back here, darling!"

He called from inside. "Be there shortly, sweetheart! Just going up to change."

She looked puzzled, but simply set his wine on a small table beside her and smiled at them. "Not sure what that's about, but he'll be quick, I'm sure. I'm assuming you're here about poor Gretchen. I'm heartbroken. She was a dear, dear friend. We had lunch the day after she arrived, and she was planning to come to book group Friday night."

"Did she seem worried when you saw her?" Demaris asked.

"Not in the slightest. She actually seemed more relaxed and content than I'd seen her in years. Her first husband, Vicky's dad, was a peach, but she hasn't fared as well since he died. I know everyone says Greg Parker was a love, but I don't think he made her happy. Poor Gretch. After that horrid Dennis Harrison, she deserved happiness. She told me she had decided to try online dating."

"Oh?"

"Yes, she just signed up before she left home. Hadn't gone on any dates yet, but she told me there were some promising matches."

"Which site was she on?"

"I think is was called Senior Singles, but Vicky would know."

"We've heard that your husband wasn't fond of Ms. Parker after she married Mr. Harrison. Was that still the case?"

"Absolutely not. Steele made his peace with that long ago."

"So you socialized together?"

"I said peace, not love. He was fine with my friendship with Gretch. Heavens, we go back sixty years. But we moved in different circles. Of course, that's true of Steele and most of my women friends. His background is a bit different than mine, plus he's a man's man, if you know what I mean."

"So if you'd invited Ms. Parker for dinner, he might make other plans?"

"Quite possible.."

"What's possible?" Steele said, stepping into the room.

At least six-four, Rubin was lean with a ruddy complexion, thick salt-and-pepper hair, and huge jutting eyebrows. He wore khakis and a pink oxford shirt, open at the neck, and boat shoes, no socks. As he stood to shake hands, Demaris wondered why their host had felt the need to change. "Mr. Rubin, Roger Demaris, RHD."

"Detective," he said, shaking his hand firmly. "Heard a lot about you last year, with the terrible death of young Harry Winthrop."

"Yes. This is my assistant, Detective Dugan."

"Hello, son," he said, shaking Pete's hand.

Pete stood and took his hand. "Sir, and it's Lieutenant Demaris. He's head of RHD."

"I see. Sorry for my mistake." Rubin could not have sounded less sorry if he had laughed in Demaris's face. "Now, what's this about possibilities?"

"I was merely inquiring about whether your antipathy toward Gretchen Parker had softened over the years."

Rubin took a seat next to his wife and sipped his wine. "My dear Lieutenant, I barely knew the woman. She was Claire's friend, not mine, so I don't have an opinion one way or the other. Claire and I led full and separate lives for almost sixty years. We each have large circles of friends with whom the other is not acquainted. We have routines and activities we enjoy with those friends separately and a few couples we see together."

"Yes, but to my knowledge, none of your friends was a contributing factor to the death of a family member of Mrs. Rubin's. I understand that when your sister, Angelina, heard of Gretchen's marriage to Dennis Harrison, she took her own life."

"Whoever told you that should be shot. My sister suffered from severe depression her entire life, exacerbated by her marriage to that monster. We were actually hopeful that when she broke free of him, there might be a chance that she would heal and be happier."

"So, hearing the news about the marriage did not drive your sister to suicide?"

"Asked and answered. My sister is none of your goddamn business anyway. Is this what you came to speak to us about? Because if yes, you can leave now and speak to my attorney."

Demaris took several deep breaths and consulted Greta's notes, which were not germane to the conversation but bought him some time. Finally, he looked up. "Gretchen Parker was one of your wife's best friends. We are here to learn what we can about the victim, which is standard practice in a homicide investigation. If you would rather step out, we can continue this conversation without you. If you stay, I would respectfully remind you that anything that relates to Ms. Parker's past is our business."

"Get on with it then, but remember, with one call I can have you off this case."

"Steele, please," Claire said. "This is not helping."

Demaris decided that ignoring their host might be the best policy, at least for a few minutes. "So, Ms. Rubin, can you think of anyone with a grudge against your friend?"

"No, she was a sweetheart. We all missed her in the book club when she and Greg moved to Florida permanently. Marge and Bob Franklin had her to dinner two nights ago. I had the impression that the evening was a bit of a strain. Bob is quite possessive and disliked most of Marge's friends. I was actually a little surprised that Gretch didn't meet her for breakfast or lunch, but she told me the evening had been his idea."

"Did you speak to her after then?"

"No, she left a message yesterday. When I tried to phone her back, her cell went right to voice mail."

"Did you save the message?"

"Oh, dear, I'm afraid I didn't. All she said was that something had upset her and she would tell me about it when we got together."

"Have you spoken to Ms. Franklin?"

"No, I emailed the book club reminder, and she responded that she'd be there. That was yesterday. I know Marge, but we're not as close friends as I was with Gretch."

"Well, thank you both." Demaris turned to Steele Rubin. "I was saying what a lovely spot this is. A wonderful place to raise children and grandchildren."

"Yes, it is." Rubin rose and filled his wine glass. Claire had barely touched hers.

"Do your children come often?"

"Yes, they love it here."

"You raised them, I understand?"

"Yes, my first wife Mindy and I raised Dennis, Lena, and Steele and always considered them ours. They have almost nothing to do with that good-for-nothing who sired them. Claire's kids Ellen and Dickie come frequently, and of course, Hollis lives with us part of each year."

Claire Rubin set down her glass and patted her husband's hand. "When Steele and I married, he kindly had an apartment put in above the garages for Hollis."

"Very generous. Must be nice to have him here."

"He's a fine young man and a scratch golfer," Rubin said.

"How did your three children feel about Gretchen Parker, Mr. Rubin?"

The abrupt change in subject startled him. His hand shook, spilling droplets of red wine on his pants. "Damn!"

Claire leapt up and grabbed a bottle of seltzer, wetting a napkin and dabbing his pants.

"Leave it!" he said, pushing her hand away.

Demaris waited silently until their hosts had settled back in their seats.

Finally, Rubin spoke. "As I said, we barely knew the woman, myself and my children."

"So they didn't blame her for their mother's death?"

"That's it. I've heard enough. I'm going to make some phone calls. Claire, I'm starved, so I hope we're eating soon."

She said nothing, but watched him go until the door slammed behind him. "I'm sorry. It's a very painful subject for Steele. He adored Angelina, you see. I knew who they were back then, but didn't know them, Steele or Mindy. They moved in very different circles than Dickie and I did, as you can imagine. Many people have told me about Angelina's troubles, though. It must be terrible to watch a loved one spiraling down and feel powerless to stop it."

"Yes," Demaris said quietly.

"Steele hates Dennis Harrison and always will, but I truly think he had made his peace with Gretchen and no longer blamed her for Angelina's suicide. After all, their marriage had broken up long before Dennis dated Gretch."

"What about his children? Had they made their peace?"

She waited several minutes, fiddling with her wine glass before replying. "I don't know. You would have to ask them. The subject is never raised, and Steele would never talk to me about it. He's very protective of them and his memories of Mindy. We try to live in the present. It's worked for us so far."

"Well, thank you, Ms. Rubin."

"Claire, please."

"Would you have contact information for Dennis Junior, Lena, and Steele Harrison?"

"Yes, let me get my address book. Be right back."

When she left the room, he turned to Pete. "We need to talk to Margery Franklin. Can you step outside and call Greta to get her information? I know where the gallery is located, but doubt it's open now."

"Will do," Pete said, setting his water glass on the bar and slipping out.

Five minutes later, Demaris thanked Claire and met Pete in the drive, finding his assistant on the phone. When Pete hung up, he turned to his boss. "Got all Franklin's info, but no one can reach her. Husband's a fisherman and he's out for the night. No answer at her home or the gallery."

"She lives in Mattapoisett, right?"

"Edge of town, main road. As the British would say—the dodgy end."

"Let's try the gallery first. Maybe she's working on something and lost track of time."

CHAPTER 22

Part of a small strip mall with a dry cleaner and barber shop on one side and a bakery and coffee shop on the on the other, Center Street Gallery's windows displayed a number of paintings, mostly seascapes and landscapes, with a small, detailed still life of beach glass occupying a prominent spot. Demaris recognized one of Palla Forest's landscapes, her style unmistakable. The gallery appeared to be closed, but when they tried the door, it swung open.

The two front rooms were empty, silent and dim in the growing twilight. At the back, a closed door had a small sign, "Private" and beside it another sign read, "No public rest room." The two men advanced, and Pete pulled down his sleeve to grasp the doorknob gingerly. It yielded, and they stepped into a small darkened space with no windows, a desk, and a few filing cabinets in the back. She was lying behind the desk, her throat partially severed by a wire still wrapped round her throat.

"Jesus Christ," Demaris said, moving to stoop beside her, feeling for a pulse that he knew he would not find. "Find a light. Then call Meg. And Pete, after that, phone the local guys. I know Chief Smith. He's a good guy and he may want this. I don't want to step on any toes."

Pete flipped a switch by the door, then stepped back into the gallery to make the calls. Demaris circled the desk, studying Margery Franklin from several angles. A few papers had fallen from the desk, suggesting there had been a struggle, but not much of one. The killer must have surprised her and been fairly strong, subduing her quickly. Her purse lay on the floor beside her, wallet and hairbrush visible. He used a pen to extract the wallet, which held at least a hundred in twenties. The rest of the office seemed untouched, except for the blood from her neck wound that had spattered on the carpet and walls around her.

Five minutes later, Paul Smith arrived with three uniformed officers, lights blazing and sirens heralding their arrival.

"Hey, Roger, it's been a while."

Not exactly handsome, the tall, slender chief was a few years older than Demaris with sharp features that had always reminded Roger of Ichabod Crane from the Washington Irving tale. His blue eyes were warm as they shook hands. Smith removed his baseball cap, revealing a thick head of sandy hair that appeared to have been cut with a chainsaw. Unlike his officers, he was in plain clothes, a flannel shirt and dark slacks.

"Paul, thanks for coming so quickly. You know her?"

"Marge? Sure, everyone knows her. She's into everything in town. My ex takes her painting classes, she volunteers at the library, and then there's this. Center Street Gallery's the most popular in town. She's good at finding local talent amidst the crap, if you know what I mean?"

He did. He had seen more than his share of cows resembling elephants and hay bales, like huge lumps of clay, dotting bucolic landscapes. "Too bad. She was a nice person."

"How'd you happen to be here?"

"We came down to talk with her in connection to a murder in Old Harbor. Gretchen Parker?"

"Been following that. They called you in, huh?"

"Away from his honeymoon, too," Pete said, stepping forward to shake Smith's hand. "Hello, sir. Nice to see you."

"Dugan, hello. How d'ya like working for RHD?"

"It's great."

"You followed your mentor, huh? You were both a loss to the village, but until the recent spate of murders, I'd have said we didn't need you in our quiet little burgs. Either way, you were both destined for greater things."

Demaris chuckled. "Don't know about that."

"So you were on your honeymoon, huh? Congratulations! I heard about that. Your pretty school teacher have any friends?"

Despite the grim pall hanging over the room, Demaris smiled. "Later, my friend. Let's grab lunch or a beer someday soon. Better get back to Margery Franklin now."

Smith studied the body, gazed round the office, and scratched his head. "It's your call, but if this relates to your investigation, I'm fine with you taking over. My guys can assist if you need us. Your forensic people on the way?"

Demaris nodded. "You sure?"

"Absolutely. I'll call and make the request. I've got great people, and the three with me can do anything you need tonight."

"Thanks, Paul. If they can secure the scene, check with surrounding shops, and see if anyone saw anybody coming or going this afternoon, including Ms.

Franklin, that would be great. Don't s'pose there'd be any surveillance cameras in this booming metropolis?"

"Funny you should ask. The dry cleaner, Mr. Chambers, is a bit paranoid. Kids were breaking his windows for fun, so he put cameras in a year ago. Only in front, though. He doesn't have a back door to the lot behind us as Marge does. You might get lucky. I can give him a call and ask him to come down if you like."

"Thanks, that'd be great. Pete, call Greta and Stevens and get 'em down here. They can work with Paul's guys."

At that moment, Demaris's cell rang, and he was surprised to see that the caller was Mary, his ex-wife. Ordinarily he would not have taken the call, but fearing something had happened to his children, he raised a finger. "Paul, sorry, I have to take this."

"No prob. Come on, Pete. I'll introduce you to Desmond, Murphy, and Mederois."

The two men stepped out of the office, and Demaris answered.

"Mary?"

"Roger? Sorry, was just about to leave a message."

"Is everything okay? Are Terry and Owen alright?"

"Yes, couldn't be better. You busy?"

He gazed out at the five men talking in the outer gallery and considered asking to call her back, but decided they were fine for five minutes without him. "I'm in the middle of a case, but I have a few minutes, or could I call you back?"

"I have a favor to ask. I'm coming to Northport next weekend. I'm bringing the kids because they really want to see you."

"Great, of course."

"You see, I've—well—this is a little awkward."

He took a few deep breaths before speaking. When he did, his voice was gentle. "Mary, I only have a few minutes. Could I call back later tonight?"

"Yes, but let me quickly tell you so you can think about this. I've…well, I've been I touch with an old friend. Boyfriend, actually. Remember Jimmy Pigeon from high school?"

He did, and the recollection was less than favorable. "Yes, vaguely."

"Well, he and I connected on Facebook, and we've been writing and talking. He's divorced and…well, one thing has led to another, and we thought we'd meet up, go out."

"Are you looking for a place to stay?"

"Oh, heavens no, not for me, at least. I'm going to stay with Paula but I thought you might take the kids?"

"Of course. I'm in the new house. Lots of boxes, but their beds are there. We can set things up by the time you arrive."

"You've sold the condo, then?"

"I told Terry and Owen that a month ago."

"So, you're married?"

"Yes, three weeks ago."

Silence.

"Mary, I really do have to go. We've just discovered a murdered woman and the team's assembling. I'd love to have the kids stay and I know Bess would, too. I'll check with her tonight and call you to confirm, okay?"

"I guess congratulations are in order?" Her voice was flat now, all emotion and dating excitement gone.

"Thanks. Shall I call later?"

"If you're sure it's okay for you to have them? A six and ten year old are not always easy."

"Completely sure. We designed the house with bedrooms for Terry and Owen in mind. We've got plenty of space."

"How nice for you both."

"Mary, I'll call later, okay?"

"Whatever. Yes, okay."

He clicked off. The bleakness of their awkward, unhappy marriage overtook him for an instant, before he spied Greta and Stevens in the gallery and smiled. His officers must have broken every speed limit to arrive so quickly. Before he could inquire about their alacrity, Pete approached, keenly aware of the change in his boss' demeanor.

"What's up, Rodge? Something wrong?"

"You mean aside from this poor dead woman? Leave it, Pete. Any sign of Meg

"They're just pulling up, boss," Greta said, eying the two men.

"Good. Let's get to work."

CHAPTER 23

Megan Krieger brushed strands of hair from her eyes as she stood, watching the stretcher take Margery Franklin away. "From the angle of the wound, the sharpness of the wire, and where the killer must have stood, it was probably quick."

Demaris nodded. "I thought as much since there's little sign of a struggle. Thanks, Meg. I'll call in the morning. It's late. Everybody go home. Chief Smith is posting a man here. Tomorrow morning I'll meet the gallery assistant and see if she notices anything amiss."

"What about you, boss?"

"I'm going to await word on the husband. If he's where they think he is, the boat won't dock till midmorning. You go home to Hillary."

"I can stay. I'm not on my honeymoon, and besides, I tell Hill to not expect me. Then, if I get home, it's a nice surprise."

"And she finds this romantic, does she?" Greta asked.

Ignoring Greta's comment, Pete grabbed his jacket. "She works just as long hours at the hospital." Hillary Dobbs was an OR nurse working at Hasbro in Providence under one of the top pediatric surgeons in the area.

"Go home, Pete. That's an order. You two as well." Demaris waved at Stevens and Greta. "I'm going out to talk to Smith's officers, and then I'll head home as soon as I hear about Bob Franklin."

"How will you get back, boss?" Pete asked.

"Chief Smith has already said Officer Murphy will drive me back. Now, go."

When his team had departed, Demaris called Bess to tell her he'd be home soon, then went to sit in the front gallery and chat with the three young officers. It wasn't long before they heard from Chief Smith. The Coast Guard had located Bob Franklin, and his estimated time back would be at least twelve hours. He said good-night to Desmond and Mederois and headed out with Shawn Murphy.

*****

Bess was waiting in the doorway when he hopped out of the squad car and thanked the young officer.

"Hello, there, stranger," she said, opening her arms.

"Good to be home."

They held each other in the light of the open door for several minutes before stepping in and closing it. "I have soup and grilled cheese. Is that okay? I can make a salad as well."

"Sounds perfect, my love."

He accepted the glass of Chianti she handed him and sat, watching her move back and forth preparing their simple supper. "How was your day?"

"Hectic, but very tame compared to yours. Students are back. Many scheduling glitches. What happened?"

"Margery Franklin was murdered."

"Oh, dear, poor Marge. Who would want to hurt her?"

"We don't know, but I cannot believe her death is not somehow connected to Gretchen Parker's."

"That's two members of the original book club!"

"Yes."

"Do you think that's the connection?"

"Too early to tell, but Dennis Harrison's involved in some way. Or at least I'd like him to be. If anyone deserves to be behind bars, it's him."

Bess smiled. "He's a miserable person, but two murders?"

"Mary called tonight."

"Oh?"

"She's coming next weekend to meet up with some old boyfriend. She wondered if the kids could stay with us."

"I hope you said yes?"

"Said I'd have to check with you."

"Roger Demaris, you are a rat. She already hates me."

He chuckled. "Just being a considerate husband."

"Baloney."

"Think we can clear out things and unpack the rooms?"

"Absolutely. I'll get started first thing tomorrow."

"Good. I'll call her and confirm after dinner."

"Will be nice to have them."

"Yes," he said, covering her hand with his. 'Thank you, my darling. I'm sorry to have to leave so early in the morning ."

"We'll have lots of mornings," she said as she set a bowl of soup and a thick grilled cheese and tomato sandwich in front of him.

Chapter 24

Carol Martin, Marge's assistant at the gallery, dabbed her eyes and waved round the gallery space. "What will we do without Marge?"

Demaris and Pete at the gallery had met Franklin's assistant at seven-thirty in the morning and she was now endeavoring to ascertain if anything was out of place, missing, or otherwise disturbed.

Demaris's phone rang, so Dugan followed the gallery assistant as she moved from room to room. "What about one of the other artists? Couldn't they take over?"

"Absolutely not! They're all useless and would run the business into the ground."

"Paul, is that you?" Demaris asked. The connection was poor and intermittent.

"Roger, I'm at the wharf. Cell phone service stinks out here. I've got bad news. Bob Franklin was hit in the head as they pulled the pots before heading back. He's pretty badly hurt. Delirious. Ambulance has taken him to Northport General."

"We'll finish up here, then head up there. Can you ask his crew to wait? I'd like my people to talk with them before they go home."

"Will do."

Demaris jotted down the boat's location, then phoned Greta and told her to pick up Stevens and get down to the wharf. He found Pete and Carol Martin in the office. She was shaking her head. "Something wrong?" he asked.

"No, not a thing. I mean, the papers are a little messy on Marge's desk, but she wasn't the neatest person. Other than that, I don't see anything funny. Would you like me to go through her desks and the closets?"

"Yes, please. I've relieved the two officers who stayed all night, but Officer Murphy will stay with you and take notes, okay? We have to go to Northport. Bob Franklin had an accident on the boat."

"Oh, dear," she said, face stricken. "Don't worry, Lieutenant, Shawn Murphy and I are good friends. We'll be fine."

*****

When they reached the hospital, they were told that Franklin was already in surgery. They grabbed coffee from the lobby snack cart, and Pete bought two donuts. "Want one, boss?"

"No, thanks. I had breakfast."

"What're you thinking?"

"That these murders are connected, but not by any thread we've pulled so far."

Finally the surgeon, Andrew Vickers, emerged. "Are you the officers waiting to see Mr. Franklin?"

"Yes, I'm Lieutenant Demaris and this is Detective Dugan. We're investigating his wife's murder."

"I heard. What a tragedy."

"How soon before we can speak to her husband?"

"Not for a while, I'm fraid. I was able to go in and relieve the pressure on Mr. Franklin's brain, but he's had a very serious head trauma. We've induced a coma to keep him still and resting."

"For how long?"

"Hard to tell. We'll monitor him and see how long before the swelling goes down. Could be a day, could be a week."

"Did he say anything when they brought him in?"

"I'm sorry. He was unconscious when he arrived."

They thanked Vickers and departed.

As Pete pulled out of the hospital lot, Demaris turned to him. "Let's stop at the clinic. I want to check in with Meg."

*****

They chatted with Krieger and her assistant for a half hour and learned little that they did not already know. "Wire is the gauge you'd use for hanging a heavy picture," Meg said.

"Readily available at a gallery," Pete said, turning over the plastic bag holding the wire.

"I would guess that it's the same kind used on Gretchen Parker. Was she involved in the gallery?"

"Only insofar as she was friends with Franklin. To my knowledge, she was not an artist," Demaris said. "What about other types of wire—for guitars or fishing or even phone wiring?"

"Maybe. We'll send it out. The gauge was similar, if not the same, is all I'm saying."

"Anything else?"

"Not much. She had paint and pigment under her nails, but no skin or other materials. If she tried to fight off her attacker, he or she must have worn gloves. We're screening for drugs. Even with a wire that cuts so efficiently, it seems like there'd have been more of a struggle."

"So, was she killed in the office?"

"Looks like it. She'd been dead about an hour or two when you found her."

"Explains why no one wandered into the gallery and found her. They close at four. Come on, Pete, let's roll. Thanks, Meg, Beth. Keep us posted."

As they made their way to the car, Dugan turned to him. "What d'ya think, Rodge?"

"I think we're dealing with an angry, calculating person who knew exactly what he or she was doing. Why these two women were murdered and what the connection is that got them killed is fuzzy, but something tells me that it's not the book club."

CHAPTER 25

Demaris took a bite of a delicious turkey sandwich, saying a silent prayer to Tilly Rogers. "So, what'd you get from the crew?"

Greta set down her egg salad wrap and picked up her notebook. "Franklin was hit with a spare anchor they keep for emergencies. His men said he was all worked up after hearing about his wife."

"Understandable."

"Yes, sir. He was running around barking orders as they pulled the last pots of the day. As the last one was released, it caught on something and swerved, crashing back along the side of the boat, dislodging the anchor from where it hung. Came right down on Franklin, hit him square in the temple. Sounds like he's lucky to be alive."

"He's not out of the woods yet. Anything else?"

Stevens cleared his throat, waiting, not wanting to interrupt his senior officer.

"Go ahead, Brendan," she said, smiling as she picked up her sandwich.

"Well, sir, one of the other men told me that Mr. Franklin was very reluctant to go out on this trip," Stevens said.

"Did he say why?" Demaris asked.

"No, but the man, Rich Sears, thought it was concern for his wife."

"Could that be hindsight given her murder?" Demaris asked.

"Partly, maybe, but Mr. Sears did say that Mr. Franklin said 'I hate to leave Marge,' or something like that."

"I don't s'pose he could be any more specific?"

"No, sir," Stevens said. "We—I mean, I—questioned him several times, and that's all he remembered. None of the four others on the boat heard anything like that."

"What'd you learn from Bill Cotter yesterday?"

"Not much," Greta said, shuffling through her notebook. "Except that everyone who was ever involved with Dennis Harrison business-wise hates the man. No one actually accused him of a crime that Cotter knows of, but they still think he's sleazy and underhanded."

"More innuendo and gossip, then."

"'Fraid so."

"What about the old boyfriend?"

"Well, I think it's safe to say that neither Brendan nor I were impressed with Mr. Harper's personality, but so far his alibi for Gretchen's murder checks out. He works at a burger joint in Northport and was there all that day. We did learn that he worked on Bob Franklin's boat three summers ago and was fired for being sloppy and lazy."

"Who told you that?"

"He did," Stevens said.

"Like I said, we weren't impressed with Mr. Harper."

"Okay, thanks, you two. Keep digging. I'd like to know where Steele Rubin really was before he met with Pete and me. I also want the dry cleaner's surveillance footage. Chief Smith is supposed to be getting that. Greta, you and Brendan take care of those things as well as canvassing the shops around the gallery. Chief Smith's men were supposed to be helping with that. I also want a complete time line of Gretchen Parker's activities for the entire time she's been here and Margery Franklin's this past week as well."

"What about us, boss?" Pete asked.

"We're also going to work on Parker's time line. I want to talk to her daughter and Suzanna Costa again. Find out where they are and make appointments to see them this afternoon, if possible. After you do that, help Greta and Brendan till I return, if you will."

"Where're you going?"

"To get a coffee and maybe a cookie at the Café on Main."

"Want me to come?"

"No, I want you to do the things I just asked you to do. I'll be back in twenty minutes."

*****

"Well, if it isn't our local boy, home at last," Betty Sue Collins said, giving Demaris a warm smile from behind the glass case of pastries and sweets.

Betty Sue and her husband, Frank, owned the Café on Main. Betty Sue was a member of the same book club as Claire Rubin and Margery Franklin. The Collins lived in a large Dutch colonial at the edge of Old Harbor Friends campus and gave generously to the town and local public schools. At least one soccer and baseball team sported Café on Main tee shirts and caps each season, and the public parks commission had received regular gifts from them over the years.

Betty Sue came from money. She grew up in the Bluffs, an exclusive enclave just down the coast from Old Harbor, and had attended boarding school, then Vassar, only to return and marry a local boy, much to her parents' dismay. Frank had grown up in Northport, had attended Babson, and had dreams of starting a business. Together they had built the very popular café and bakery, which had a reputation that reached far beyond the tiny village. It was a favorite breakfast and lunch spot. People traveled for miles to sit at one of the cheerful blue-and-white-striped tables indoors, or outdoors in the summer months.

"Didn't I hear you were on your honeymoon?" Betty Sue asked.

"Something like that," Demaris said. "How are you, Bet?"

"Been better. Losing two friends in one week isn't much fun."

"I'm sorry for your loss."

"Thanks. You hungry, or is this an official visit?"

"A little of both. Got a minute?"

"For you, anytime. Coffee?"

"Iced, cream, three sugars, thanks."

She waved to a young woman clearing tables. "Barb, come take over here. Get Jerry to do that if you would, please."

The blonde teenager disappeared momentarily, then reappeared minus her soiled apron, followed by a tall, gangly male about her age who carried rags and a bucket.

"You're looking well. Marriage must suit you," Betty Sue said, setting down his iced coffee and sipping on what appeared to be iced tea. A little older than him, she had reddish-brown hair, probably dyed, bright brown eyes, and rosy cheeks. Betty Sue Collins also had a smile that would melt an iceberg, which many said was the major reason for the Café's success.

"It does. You're looking good, too, Bet. How's Frank?"

"You know Frank. Same ole, same ole. He's running errands. Be back soon."

"How you holding up?"

"Horrible. All of us have been in shock."

"Had you seen Gretchen on this visit?"

"Yes, we had breakfast Tuesday, two days after she arrived. Frank opened up so we could stay at my house and catch up. Poor Gretch. She was finally pulling her life together. She was happier than I'd seen her in a while. Had plans to see so many friends this week, and of course, she was planning to come to book club this week."

"Will you still meet?"

She nodded. "Not to discuss the book, but we're catering for Gretch's memorial, and now, I imagine, poor Margery's as well. We thought we should get together and plan a little. We, Frank and I, will do all the pastries, but the ladies will fill in with salads, sandwiches, appetizers. The café could have done it all, but this is how it's done in the village. Everyone likes to pitch in."

"Will be a comfort to Vicky and Suzanna to have you there."

"Yes, Vicky's thanked us a million times already and Suzanna's serving. Her brother, Barry, has agreed to act as bartender."

"Barry? I didn't know he lived here."

"He doesn't, but apparently he's visiting for a few weeks. Not one of my favorite people, but Suz says he has lots of serving experience. I was going to ask Charlie Boardman, but he's working, and it might ruffle Tilly's and Rachel's feathers if I took him away on a busy fall Sunday."

"How often does Suzanna work for you?"

"Two afternoons a week and usually one weekend day. She also helps out with special functions."

"What days did she work this past week?"

"Hmm, let me think. I know she was here Tuesday, from about four to closing. Helped Frank start Wednesday's baking. I think that was it. She was supposed to work Thursday, but she cancelled and rushed home to be with poor Vicky."

"Did Gretchen express concern about anything?"

"Not when I saw her, but Claire said she was a bit agitated when they spoke Tuesday night. I think she was planning to chat with her before book group."

"How well do you know Dennis Harrison?"

"Better than I'd like. We saw quite a bit of him when he and Gretchen were married, but after the divorce, not at all unless we bumped into him. He lives in Florida now and isn't around much. When he's in town, he comes for coffee many mornings and chats with Frank. Knows better than to bother me. Can't stand the man."

"Did you know his children?"

"Not really. Steele Junior comes in once and a while, if he has a local landscaping job. His wife Lizzy works at Old Harbor Friends, you know."

"Yes, nice young woman," he said."

"Anyway, Harrison's kids grew up in Mattapoisett and were long gone before Claire married Steele. We still miss dear Dickie."

"Yes, he was a great guy. Is their relationship with their stepmother cordial?"

"Gee, I don't know. You'd have to ask Claire. She rarely talks about Steele or the kids, except her own. Steele is not the warmest person, and he's very private."

"Did you know his first wife?"

"Not at all. We weren't in the same social circles, I'm afraid. From all reports, she was warmer than him."

"Dennis Harrison left quite a trail of broken hearts in his wake, didn't he?"

"You can say that again. Poor Gretch. It took her years to get over him."

"What about Margery Franklin?"

"So you know about Marge, then?" He nodded. "That was a very brief affair. Happened before he married Gretchen, after his divorce from Angelina."

"Were there others upon whom Harrison preyed?"

"You're thinking of Lee, aren't you?"

"Lee Myers?"

"Yes, she and Dennis had a brief fling while he was still married to Angelina. It was during one of Lee's really low periods when her brute of a husband had disappeared. Dennis wooed her when she was most vulnerable. Hurt her terribly, and she paid dearly when Jack came back and heard about it."

"Where is Jack now?"

"I think he lives in Taunton, but honestly, I don't know. He was a dreadful person. We're all convinced that Lee's horrible marriage, then the business with Dennis, hastened her poor brother's demise. Dickie always tried to help, but Lee was adamant that she could handle things herself."

"I hear she's dating again?"

"Was dating a UMass professor, but from what I hear, it's kind of on-again, off-again. She's been experimenting a bit with the online dating, too."

"Well, thanks, Bet. I'll let you get back to work. Say hi to Frank."

"Will do." She gave him a hug and disappeared into the kitchen.

He nearly ran into Frank Collins on the sidewalk. The café owner was laden with boxes and bags. Frank set his load on the ground and extended his hand. "Hey, the conquering hero has come home! Heard you were back. Living in town again, too. Good to see you."

"You, too, Frank," he said, genuinely glad to see the other. There were so many good people in Old Harbor, and the Collinses were two of them.

"How's tricks?"

"Pretty good, although this week's been rough."

"Poor gals. Great ladies, both of them. Bet's been devastated."

"Yes, I'm sure. To lose two good friends in one week."

"Any progress findin' the bastard or bastards?"

"Not yet. Can you think of any connection between the two women?"

"Not really. I mean, Bet was fretting that someone was killing off their book group, but I doubt that's the connection. There's the Harrison connection, of course. Both Gretchen and Marge were romantically involved with Dennis. If that's the connection, my Bet is safe. Aside from a girlish crush on the former headmaster at OHF, she's been faithful, as far as I know."

"Betty Sue had a crush on Peter Thurbert?"

Collins laughed. "Only a schoolgirl crush. Should've seen her the first year he arrived. 'What can I get you, Peter? So glad to see you, Mr. Thurbert. Can I recommend the scones today?' Was quite a show."

"Sounds like good service to me."

"Had to be there to see it. It was all in the delivery. Only lasted a while. Then she decided he was snobby and aloof."

Demaris chuckled. "She wasn't far off. Well, gotta go. Good to see you. If you or Betty Sue think of anything that might help, let me know."

"Congratulations on your wedding, by the way. Bet and I were so pleased for both of you."

"Thanks, Frank. That means a lot."

CHAPTER 26

"Hey, Meg, this is a surprise," Demaris said, stepping into the guest house to find his forensic pathologist lounging on the sofa, reading a magazine.

"Had a few things to share, and I wanted you to have this." She tossed a plastic evidence baggie on the coffee table. It held a small length of wire. "Just in case you find any lying around. This is probably what he or she used for the garrote.

"And?"

"And, we found threads of this wire in the carpet of Margery Franklin's office. It was cut there, probably after she was garroted."

"So you're thinking it was wrapped around something?"

"Pretty sure, or the ends wouldn't be straight the way they are. There'd be curling in order for the killer to get a good grip. I'm guessing the wire was wrapped or secured in some way to pieces of wood or something."

"Like those industrial cheese slicers."

"Exactly. And this wire matches wire used for industrial cheese slicers. It's culinary wire."

"Can you say with certainty that this type of wire killed Gretchen Parker, too?"

"Not yet, but the wounds are so similar that it's a good guess."

"Sounds ritualistic."

"Maybe. Oh, and Franklin had diazepam in her system, probably mixed into the smoothie we found traces of in her stomach. Coconut-strawberry-banana smoothie. No diazepam in her office or purse, so I'm guessing the killer brought it."

"I'll ask Chief Smith if his men can search her house."

"How's the husband doing?"

"Still in a coma."

"Poor man."

"Meg, have you been home?"

"Not for two days."

"Then go home."

"Thanks, boss. I'll be back in the morning if you need me."

After calling Chief Smith to request a search of the Franklin house, Demaris sat back on the sofa and closed his eyes. Just as he opened them, Pete appeared, Greta and Stevens with him.

"Hey, boss," Greta said. "We're headin' down to Mattapoisett now, unless you need us. Carol Martin's gonna meet us at the dry cleaner's next to the gallery. Owner claims his machine is the only one that can play the video, but we'll see when we get there. Bring it back if we can."

"I'll call and get a warrant. I want that tape and whatever equipment we need to play it. Try to get an accounting of Marge's activities the day she died, would you?"

"Will do." Greta grabbed her shoulder bag and headed for the back door leading to the cottage's driveway. Stevens nodded and smiled before following her out. Pete grabbed a water from the fridge and sat across from him.

"Where are we, Pete? Tell me something encouraging."

"We're meeting Vicky Brown at the condo at three-thirty," Dugan said. "Suzanna's working, but she said that late afternoons are pretty slow. They close at five and are mostly prepping for the morning. She said to just stop by the café after we talk to Vicky. Steele Rubin was MIA from the time he left his office yesterday, shortly after lunch, until he appeared at the house."

"According to whom?"

"His wife, coworkers. I called the bar at the golf club where he sometimes hangs out or stops by for a drink, but no one remembers seeing him. Want me to stop by there later?"

"Leave it for now. I'd like to talk to him again."

"Well, you're in luck. We just saw him and his wife heading into the Tavern."

"Were they alone?"

"Nope. Lee Myers and a man we didn't recognize were with them."

Demaris checked his watch. It was almost two. "You stay here. I'll be back in five minutes."

Before Pete could protest, he headed out the door and closed it behind him. As he closed the taproom's back door, he spied the foursome seated by the window. He headed their way, stopping to ask Rachel if someone could take their order as soon as they were ready.

"Of course. Anything for you, handsome."

"Thanks, Rach. I'll give you a nod."

Lee spotted him first and smiled. "Hello, Lieutenant. Nice to see you."

He nodded. "Ms. Myers, Rubins, sorry to intrude."

Steele Rubin glared at him. "Then don't."

Claire gave her husband a look, which he ignored.

In the awkward silence, Lee said, "I don't believe you've met my friend, Larry Goodman."

"No. Hello."

Goodman stood and they shook hands. "I've heard a lot about you."

"Larry teaches at UMass," Lee said.

"Oh, what department?"

"Biology," he said, taking his seat.

Lee was a slim, athletic woman with salt-and-pepper hair and gray-blue eyes, and she beamed as she looked at her friend. She was dressed casually, as was he. Both were in jeans, Lee in a blue marled sweater, Goodman in a navy fleece with the UMass logo. He looked younger than her by maybe ten years.

"Is this why you came over, to meet Lee's boyfriend?" Rubin snarled.

"Steele, that's enough."

"No, actually it's you I came to see, Mr. Rubin," Demaris said, voice low. "May I ask that after you order you accompany me over to the guest house for a quick conversation?"

"You can ask, but the answer is no."

"Okay, then. I will have one of my officers pick you up in the morning and escort you to RHD. We can speak there. You would be welcome, of course, to bring your attorney. It shouldn't take more than a few hours."

Rubin threw down his napkin. "Jesus Christ, let's go. Claire, order me a Reuben, large Tilly's tea, fries, and cole slaw. I'll be back in five minutes. This had damn well better be good."

Rubin stalked on ahead of Demaris and shoved the door of the guest house so hard that it slammed against the wall. Pete's eyes widened. He would not have been surprised to see steam shooting out of Rubin's ears, but his boss appeared calm and cool.

"Have a seat, Mr. Rubin. Can Pete get you something to drink?" Demaris said.

Rubin took one of the dining table chairs, leaned back, and crossed his arms. "Not unless you have Scotch on the rocks."

"I'll take that as a no, then." Demaris took a seat across from him and made eye contact with Pete, who immediately moved to a chair at the far end of the table. "We won't keep you long, but we need an accounting of your whereabouts the afternoon before we visited with you, and also your activities yesterday. An honest accounting. If you are forthcoming, this can be very quick. Or, as I said a few minutes ago, you can make an appointment to come to our RHD office in Taunton and make a formal statement with your attorney present."

"Not that it's any of your goddamn business, but I was working all day Thursday, and same until Claire and I spoke with you yesterday."

"Not according to your building staff. They told my detectives you were not in the office at all Thursday and that you left around one-thirty yesterday."

"This is outrageous! How dare you check into my affairs."

"This is a homicide investigation, Mr. Rubin. We check into everyone's affairs, especially those persons who may have had a strong motive."

"And what could my motive possibly be?"

"Hatred, because these women were involved with your former brother-in-law and could have contributed to your sister's suicide."

"Look, I don't like women who go out with married men. I consider them floozies of the worst sort, but as far as I know, both Gretchen Parker and Marge Franklin were dallying with that asshole *after* he broke my sister's heart."

"Well, then, once you give us an accounting of your whereabouts, you can get back to lunch."

"I told you, I was working. I often work away from the office, meet clients for lunch, drinks, at their offices, whatever."

"So is that what you've been doing the past few days?"

"Yes."

"Well, that clears things up. If you can give Detective Dugan the names and contact information for these clients, and where you met with them, we're done."

"Listen, Demaris, I've been patient and polite, but this is harassment. My clients expect confidentiality."

"Then perhaps you can provide me with your attorney's name. After the warrant is issued, my assistant from RHD will be in touch with you both to set up tomorrow's meeting." Demaris stood. "You're free to go back to lunch now."

"Wait a second. Jesus Christ, okay, okay. If I tell you something, does it stay here?"

"If it does not compromise the investigation, we will keep your private life private."

"I was with a woman."

"I take this is an amorous relationship of which your wife is unaware?"

"Yes." Rubin stared at the floor, all the fight knocked out of him.

"We'll need the name and contact information for your lady friend."

"Is that absolutely necessary?"

Demaris remained silent, eyes riveted to Rubin's.

"Okay, fine, whatever," Rubin said. "It's Carol Martin."

"The gallery assistant?"

"Yes. I'm sure you have her contact info."

"Yes, we do. If both of you had been forthcoming, we would not have wasted so much time." Demaris let irritation slip into his voice, but mostly he was angry.

He liked Claire Rubin. She deserved better. "You can go, Mr. Rubin." He grabbed a file of papers and began flipping through them, ignoring their visitor completely.

"So, I'm dismissed, I guess?" Rubin rose. At the door, he turned back. "It just happened, you know? I love my wife. It means nothing."

"Have you told Ms. Martin that?"

"Fuck you!"

He slammed behind him.

"What an asshole," Pete muttered, watching his boss clench and unclench his jaw.

"Where does Carol Martin live?"

"Rents one of the condos near Osprey Point."

"Find her and tell her we need to see her today. Five would be perfect. Try to get her in here. Stevens can pick her up, if necessary."

"What're you gonna do?"

"Make a quick call to my bride. Then we can head out to talk to Costa."

*****

"Roger? Hi, are you okay?"

"Yes, my love. Just needed to hear your voice. Not in class?"

"All done for the day. I have a quick meeting. Then Joan and I thought we might go out and paint at the bluffs." She referred to her colleague, Joan Nettleman, the middle school art teacher. "Such a beautiful day. Unless…are you coming home?"

"Home. I love the sound of that. No, 'fraid not. Will try to make it in time for dinner. Can I pick something up?"

"No, I'll cook. Maybe fish?"

"Perfect."

"You sound a little down."

"Uncovering too many skeletons."

"Can I help?"

"I hesitate to ask this, because I do not want you involved, but if you're able to bring up either of the victims, Parker or Franklin, with your colleagues, any background might be helpful. Steele Rubin or Dennis Harrison, too. Don't push, but see what you can learn."

"I don't know either of the men well, although I know Claire, of course. Gretchen and Marge only slightly, but I'll see what the campus grapevine yields."

"Only with people you trust, Bess. Only with friends."

"Will do. Take care, Roger, please."

"You, too. I love you."

"I love you, too, darling husband."

When he clicked off, he found Pete right behind him. "Okay, nosy Parker, let's go. Did you get a hold of Carol Martin?"

"Yup, she'll meet us here at five. Thinks it's about the gallery."

"Good."

CHAPTER 27

Just as they pulled into the parking lot at The Glen, Demaris's cell rang. "Hey, boss," Greta said. "Got a minute?

"Of course. What d'ya got?"

"Mattapoisett cops searched the Franklin house. No diazepam or any kind of drug except an old prescription for amoxicillin. We've got the dry cleaner's tape and the machine to play it on, and we're heading back now."

"Great. Thanks, Greta. We've asked Carol Martin to come in at five. I'm sure Pete and I'll be back by then, but if not, have her view the video and identify anyone she knows."

"Will do."

He rung off and they headed up to the second floor condo of Vicky Brown and Suzanna Costa. Pete knocked and the door was opened by a stranger. "Hey, you must be the cops. Suz is just gettin' outta the shower. Come in. I'm her brother, Barry."

They introduced themselves and followed the short, dark-haired man into the living room. "Nice afternoon. You guys wanta sit out on the deck?"

"Anywhere is fine," Demaris replied, marveling at the man's muscular arms that were completely covered with tattoos. While they weren't horrendous, they were far from professional. If he had to guess, he'd say they were prison tattoos. What had he heard about Barry Costa?

"Okay, I'll let Suz decide. Can I get you something to drink? Beer? Soda? Water?"

"Thank you, but we're fine."

"Then I'll leave you to it. I'm working in the den. Yell if you need something. Suz'll be out momentarily."

They stood at the slider leading to the deck, gazing out at the creek running alongside the property. It was the same view Pete and Hillary had. Peaceful and serene.

Several minutes later, she appeared in pink sweats, a towel wrapped round her head, which she removed to reveal dry hair. She combed it back with her fingers as she threw the towel over the back of the couch. "Hi. Let's sit outside, okay? I've been cooped up with middle schoolers all day. I need fresh air. Did Barry offer you something to drink?"

"Yes, thanks." Demaris said, pulling back the glass slider to allow her to pass.

"Vicky should be home soon. She's talking with the Clerk of the Meeting. We're having the service on the campus, at the Meeting House. Kevin LeBlanc's a friend," She said, referring to one of the Old Harbor Friends teachers. "He helped Vicky arrange it."

She sat at one of four wrought iron chairs ringing a circular table, and they took the two opposite her.

"Thanks for seeing us, Suzanna. We won't be long," Demaris said.

"Of course. Anything to help. Poor Vick. She's understandably devastated by her mom's death, but she was pretty close to Marge, too. When Gretchen moved to Florida, Marge became sort of a surrogate mom to Vick. Always checking in, taking her to lunch, inviting us for dinner."

"That was kind of her."

"Yes, she was a sweetheart. We aren't as crazy about Bob. He's a little rough around the edges, but he adored Marge as we did. How's he doing, anyway?"

"Well, as far as I know, they're hoping to bring him out of the coma soon."

"Poor guy. He's gonna be lost without Marge."

"Suzanna, we wanted to speak with you again because you told my detectives during your first interview that Lee Myers was involved with Dennis Harrison?"

"Yes, just like almost every woman of a certain age from here to Timbuktu."

"They also said that you had little nice to say about Mr. Harrison. Can you elaborate on the origin of your feelings?"

"Well, for one thing, he screwed Gretchen over big time. Spent her money, stole things and sold them, and treated her like shit. Gretchen was like a mother to me. I hated to see her hurt."

"Were you and Vicky friends during her mother's marriage to Harrison?"

"We've been friends since high school. I went through the tail end of Harrison, then Greg Parker, and most recently online dating with mother and daughter. Gretchen was just dipping her toes into the online stuff. Lee was encouraging her, I think. Vick and I do online dating on and off, so it was pretty funny, sharing stories with her mom."

"And had she been successful?"

"Not yet. She just created her profile and went on about a week or so ago. I know she hadn't had a date yet, but I'm not sure whether she'd been corresponding with anyone. Senior Singles works slightly differently than the sites Vick and I use."

"What, if anything, can you tell me about Dennis Harrison's children?"

"Not much, except they were not close. That was Dennis's fault in the early days, from what I understand, but Claire's stick-up-the-ass husband, Steele Rubin, didn't help."

"Oh?"

"According to Vicky and Gretchen, Steele took every available opportunity to trash Dennis's reputation with his kids. Not that Dennis needed any help. He did a pretty good job trashing himself."

"Did you know any of them?"

"They're much older than Vick and me, but I've met Lena and Steele a few times. She's not Stella McCartney, but she's a talented designer and her shop's pretty successful. You see Steele around sometimes with his landscaping trucks. Wouldn't know Dennis Junior if I saw him. He was away at boarding schools, camps, and then college when Gretchen was with Dennis, and even when he was home, they didn't get together much."

"Have you seen any of them recently?"

"Actually, now that you mention it, I saw Steele's truck in town this past week. Not sure which day."

"What was he doing?"

"The truck was parked on Main Street. Probably stopped for coffee and muffins before heading to a job."

"So it was morning then?'

"Think so. The middle school had a professional day Thursday, so I went a little later than usual. Yup, that's when I saw him, on my way to school."

"Well, thanks, Suzanna. We'll let you go. Is your brother here to stay?"

She laughed. "Barry never stays anywhere long. He's here for a week or two, trying to make some money. He alternates between here and a friend's place in Northport. He'll be tending bar for the reception after Gretchen's funeral."

They said their good-byes and headed out. When they reached the car, Demaris turned to Pete. "I want everything you can find out about Barry Costa. I bet a week's salary those are prison tattoos. Let's find out where he got them."

Chapter 28

"Carol Martin identified all the people on the video, mostly regular customers," Greta said, as all four of them viewed the dry cleaner's grainy security footage.

"And her lover," Pete said as the team watched Steele Rubin enter the gallery.

"Who?" Greta asked, staring at Pete.

"Martin and Rubin were doin' the nasty," Pete said, leaning back in his chair and receiving a disapproving look from his boss.

"Poor Claire," she said. "Does she know?"

"We don't think so," Demaris said as Stevens fast-forwarded the tape. The last person who entered was a young man, whom Stevens identified as Sonny Wilkerson. He worked part-time for Margery, cleaning the gallery.

"Would you three like to order dinner?" Demaris asked. "I'm going to try to get home after we talk to Carol Martin, but you can put in your orders with Tilly."

"Hill's making chili so I'm headed home," Pete said. "You guys are welcome to come. She always makes gallons."

"Count me in," Greta said.

Stevens nodded. "Sure, thanks, if it's not too much trouble?"

A knock at the back door sent Stevens to open it.

"Greta, can you and Brendan assemble any notes you've made about the activities of Parker and Franklin on the day they died?" Demaris asked. "Harrison, too. Pete, before you sit down with us, please step out and call Lee Myers. I want to talk with her in the morning."

"Will do, boss."

After their visitor entered, Greta and Stevens retreated to the kitchen area and Pete stepped out the other door to make the call. Demaris stood to greet Carol Martin.

"Ms. Martin, thank you for coming on such short notice. We won't keep you long. Can we offer you something to drink?"

"No, I'm fine, thank you."

"Shall we, then?" He indicated the chairs and love seat at the far end of the room. With a glance at Greta and Stevens at the kitchen counter, she hurried across the room and sat on the love seat. Demaris took one of the upholstered chairs at her side.

Martin appeared to be in her midthirties, her shoulder-length ash-blond hair straight and tucked behind her ears. She wore tight designer jeans, a beige fitted cotton jacket, and a multicolored scarf round her long, slender neck. She was pretty but unremarkable except for sparkling brown eyes, which appeared to be on the verge of tears.

"Nice to see you again. As I said at the gallery, I am sorry for your loss. Had you worked for Ms. Franklin for long?"

"Fifteen years. She took me on right after college. I love the gallery. It's only part-time, of course, since Marge couldn't afford to pay much, but it was my passion."

"Do you have other jobs?"

"Yes, I work as a bookkeeper for a number of local businesses, and I'm also a writer."

"Oh?"

"Beach romances. They sell moderately well in local shops. I've got five. They're all self-published."

"Good for you."

"Is this why you wanted to see me? To ask about my work? I believe I told your detectives and the Mattapoisett police everything I know about Marge's activities the day she died."

Pete returned and took the seat opposite his boss, notebook in hand.

Demaris gave Carol a warm smile. "We're very appreciative of all your information, Ms. Martin. Very helpful. No, I wanted to talk with you about your relationship with Steele Rubin."

The color drained from her face as she clapped her hand over her mouth. "Oh, God."

"You are not in any trouble, Ms. Martin. We are just trying to establish people's whereabouts on Wednesday and Thursday. Mr. Rubin has told us he was with you Wednesday for most of the day, and then again yesterday afternoon."

She nodded. "Wednesday's my day off. Weeks ago, we planned an outing to Osprey Point. I live near there. Steele ordered a lovely picnic. Then we went back to my condo. Yesterday I was through with work at noon, and we met at my place again."

"What time was that?"

"I think he arrived about two, maybe two-thirty."

"And when did Mr. Rubin leave your place?"

"Why? Is he a suspect?"

"We're checking everyone's whereabouts, who might have had a connection to Ms. Parker or Ms. Franklin."

"To my knowledge, he barely knew either woman, although he's bought the occasional painting from the gallery. I would guess he left me shortly after four. Said he had to get home to meet with you, I believe."

"How long has your affair been going on?"

Martin looked stricken and stared down at her hands. "About six months. I feel awful about it, but I love him. He keeps saying he's going to leave Claire."

"And you believe him?"

She shook her head. "I'm not stupid, Lieutenant. Steele Rubin's a player. Always has been. I knew his reputation and went into this with my eyes wide open. I was just sick of being alone, and the eligible guys around here are few and far between."

"Are you saying that Rubin has had other affairs?"

"Duh! Cheated on his saint of a wife Mindy for years, and now Claire. I can't believe Claire didn't know about him when she married him."

"Do you know any of his previous lovers?"

"He likes 'em young. He's rumored to have had an affair with that roommate of Gretchen Parker's daughter. You'd have to check the Mattapoisett rumor mill for the rest. Steele doesn't keep any of us around long."

"Suzanna Costa?"

"Yup, but it might not be true. That was the gossip a few years ago, though. About a year after he married the current Mrs. Rubin."

"Well, thank you, Ms. Martin. May I say that I believe you deserve better."

"Damn right I do, but he'll move on soon. He gives really nice presents," she said, holding up her slender wrist to reveal a delicate diamond and gold bracelet. "I checked. This cost almost ten thousand dollars. Think I can sell it on eBay?"

"Take care, Ms. Martin. Good night."

When she had closed the door behind her, Greta looked up from her computer. "Jeez Louise, is there anyone around here not having an affair?"

Demaris smiled wearily as she handed him several file folders. He then turned to Pete. "What'd you arrange with Lee Myers?"

"She'll meet us here at nine tomorrow morning."

"Okay—go enjoy Hillary's chili. I'll see everyone back here at eight. I'll eat at home, but anyone who wants to order breakfast should check in with Tilly tonight or before eight, comprende?"

CHAPTER 29

Because it was a warm night, he had suggested they take their wine and cheese and sit out on the terrace for the first time, two Adirondack chairs facing the fields and ocean beyond. "Heaven," he said, sinking back in the chair, feeling the familiar divots and cracks from years of use on his deck. They were among the few things he had kept from his house, then stored during his years in the condo. He had been afraid Bess would reject them as ramshackle and past their prime, but his wife loved what he loved and insisted they come. Years ago he had bought the chairs from a local farmer, who had since passed away. Every season, he rubbed them with linseed oil so that they now had a warm, smooth patina.

She reached out and took his hand. "Roger, thank you for this."

"Wine on the terrace?"

"You know what I mean. Thank you for agreeing to build here."

"I told you already, I didn't care where we built or where we lived as long as we are together. If this makes you happy, then I'm more than content. As you know, I'm very fond of Mr. Winthrop and I'd grown to like his son, too."

"Harry was rather in awe of you, did I ever tell you that? There wasn't anyone he respected more."

"I doubt that."

"Harry might have acted capricious, but underneath he was very serious, and he admired expertise and intelligence."

He squeezed her hand. "Now, you're flattering me, wife of mine. Did you burn the fish or something?"

She sat up, looking over at him. "I'm serious, Roger, and no, I did not burn the fish!"

Later, over dinner, she told him about the day's conversations with her colleagues. "Most people didn't know Gretchen Parker. Vicky didn't go to Old Harbor Friends. Kevin LeBlanc says that Vicky and Suzanna are gym rats. They take a bunch of Sue LeBlanc's classes. Joan didn't have much to contribute, although she did say that Dennis Harrison hit on her a number of times over the years."

He chuckled, picturing Bess's colleague in the art department with Dennis Harrison. "In her dreams."

"Joan used to be gorgeous, very slim and stylish. It's only in the last ten years or so that she's let herself go a bit."

"What about Steele Rubin? Did he ever hit on her or anyone at school?"

"It's funny you should ask that, because Kevin said that when he and Sue were still married, she would get really aggravated by Steele's flirting."

"Pot calling the kettle black."

She laughed. "Sue didn't develop her vamp act until after the divorce."

"Could've fooled me," he said, thinking back to Sue LeBlanc's shameless flirting during a previous investigation. "So who from school will be at the service?"

"I know Kevin and Sue plan to go, and Jane and Joan. I imagine Pru will be there, and Peter and Carrie Thurbert. I bumped into Garrett Rollins on my way out today, and he says he's going."

"Oh?"

"Not sure what the connection is. Oh, and not that it's relevant, but Joan went on and on about how much she despises Palla Forest. She and Clarice are friends, but she claims Palla is unethical in her artwork."

"In what way?"

"I'm not sure. We got interrupted at that point, but Joan is always on the lookout for plagiarism and artists copying each other's work."

As they washed and dried the dishes, working side by side in companionable silence, he stopped, set down his dish towel, and circled his arms round her waist, head on her shoulder. "I love you."

"Love you, too," she whispered, as his cell phone vibrated on the counter.

Reluctantly, he reached for it. "This better be good, Pete."

"We've got a situation here, boss. Thought you'd want to know."

"What's up?"

"We're at Lee Myers's house. She's scared shitless."

"Has she been hurt?"

"No, but she's real shaken up."

"I'll be there in five minutes."

Bess watched him, the relaxed face of her husband gone, replaced by the face he showed the world. "What's happened?"

"Something has frightened Lee Myers. I'll go check things out and be back soon."

"Would you like me to come with you?"

"No, thanks, darling. You go to bed." He kissed her softly, then grabbed his jacket from the peg by the back door.

"Be careful."

"Always."

*****

When he arrived at the cottage on the north edge of campus, the only car visible was Pete's. Then he remembered that Lee Myers did not drive and hadn't for many years. It was a personal choice based on a combination of poor eyesight and fear of the road. She bicycled locally and used buses, cabs, and student drivers for the remainder of her transportation needs.

As Demaris headed up the walk, a third car drove up and Larry Goodman, the erstwhile boyfriend, jumped out. "How is she?"

"Just getting here. Let's find out, shall we?"

They stepped into the living room, where they found Pete and Stevens standing, while Greta sat beside Lee on the sofa. Lee was drinking what appeared to be tea. "Oh, Larry," she cried, leaping up and flinging herself into her boyfriend's arms.

"Okay, hon, you're safe now." Goodman embraced her looking vaguely uncomfortable.

"Ms. Myers, I'm going to step outside with my detectives for a few minutes," Demaris said. "Then I'll come back and talk with you, okay?"

She nodded, still clinging desperately to Goodman, who now resembled a caged animal.

On the stoop, they closed the door behind them, and he turned to Pete. "What the hell happened?"

"She was coming back from her Pilates class at the Harbor Gym, and she thought someone was following her. She kept looking back, but there was no one there. Then, about two blocks from home, she heard footsteps running. Before she knew it, she'd been knocked down and someone had wrapped something around her neck. Fortunately, she screamed and a couple of the Old Harbor Friends kids came running. We suspect they'd been out behind the wall, smoking pot. Anyway, they scared off Myers's attacker, but saw nothing. Found her lying alone on the sidewalk, gym bag flung in the street."

"Jesus Christ, we should have had someone watching her," Demaris said, the weight of his mistake like a blow to the chest.

"I can stay, sir," Stevens said, stepping forward into the light.

"Not alone, you can't. Pete, call Skeeter and Vance. See if one or both of them are available. If yes, have them get down here ASAP." Skeeter Morris and Vance Gibney were part-time RHD employees who did crime scene work and lent support to investigations when needed. Each had several other part-time jobs but were usually flexible enough to shuffle things when needed.

Pete stepped away to make the call as Greta and Stevens followed him back into the house. They found Goodman and Myers sitting side by side on the sofa, his arm round her shoulders. "Mr. Goodman, I wonder if you would step into the kitchen to chat with my officers for a few minutes. I'd like to talk with Ms. Myers alone."

Goodman jumped up, the relief on his face almost comical.

"Anything you have to say to me, you can say with Larry present."

"I'm sure that's true," Demaris said, voice gentle. "But this is standard procedure. It will only take a few minutes, I promise. Then you and Larry can be together."

"I'll be right out here, hon," Larry said, practically sprinting from the room.

Myers gazed at the closed kitchen door, then turned to face Demaris. "As you can see, my relationship with Larry is rather one-sided. I give it another month, maybe less."

"There are other men out there."

"That's easy for you to say."

He walked her through the description of the attack, which aligned with Pete's. When they finished, she was trembling.

"Lee, I want to ask you something unrelated to tonight. It's about your relationship with Dennis Harrison."

"Ancient history. Yet another example of my failed, horrendous relationships."

"When was this?"

"I'm ashamed to say that it was when he was still married to Angelina. Jack, my husband, had walked out, and I met Dennis one night at the Tavern, having a drink in the taproom. He turned on the charm and seemed so concerned for my welfare, so understanding, blah, blah, blah. Angelina was away, having one of her periodic mental health vacations. When things got really bad, her brother, Steele, would intervene and take her out to The Red Door. It's a ritzy spa in the Berkshires with therapists and psychiatrists on staff. She'd usually stay for a month or two, get her head back on straight, then come home."

"Did she know about you and Dennis?"

"I don't think so. Our fling was over by the time she got back. He told me he had to stand by Angelina until she was stronger. Then we could explore our future together. Such bullshit, excuse my language. He was already on to someone new, I'm sure."

"Do you know who?"

"No, but Dennis has a really short attention span."

"Lee, I'm sorry this happened to you tonight, but I'm concerned that you may have been targeted because of your time with Harrison. It seems to be the one thing that connects you with Ms. Franklin and Gretchen Parker."

"Aside from the fact that we are all members of the same book club."

"Yes, that's true. I'm going to place two bodyguards here tonight. You won't see them, but they'll be outside."

"I'm sure that's not necessary. Larry will probably agree to stay."

"Even so, they'll be there. Are you attending Gretchen Parker's service?"

"Yes."

"I'll see you there, then. Good night. Take care."

CHAPTER 30

"Here we are again, sir," Greta said as she and Demaris stood outside the Meeting House, perched at the highest point on campus. "You in your gorgeous suit and me in my Armani knock-off."

"Might be a knock-off, but you sure look like a knockout," he said, smiling at his third-in-command. Her dark gray suit hugged every curve, its short pencil skirt revealing beautiful legs. "No hat today?"

Greta laughed. "Would have spoiled the look."

As usual, Stevens wore what his mentor wore, his dark gray suit and blue dress shirt almost identical to Pete's. Their ties were the only differentiating feature. Both wore black department-issue shoes, polished to a sheen. They stood in the shadows just inside the building as mourners filed in.

Demaris smiled, sharing a private look with Bess as she walked by with Jane Fellows and Joan Nettleman.

"Bess looks gorgeous," Greta said as they disappeared.

"Always."

"Yes, but that's a new look for her, huh?" she said, referring to the light gray suit, set off with a silk blouse and heels and a stylish matching hat.

"Her mother took her shopping before the wedding."

"Maggie does have style," Greta said, referring to his wife's thrice-married mother.

"That she does."

"Hello, Lieutenant. How are you?" Pru Marsden was dressed in a black tweed suit and red silk scarf, her snow-white hair was perfectly coifed. She reached out and shook his hand.

"Hello, Ms. Marsden. Not sure if you've met my detective, Greta Burke?"

"No, it's a pleasure. This is my husband, Philip Randolph."

Demaris, then Greta, shook both their hands. "Good to meet you, Mr. Randolph."

"Phil, please."

"I understand you do a lot of traveling."

"Yes, just got back from third trip to Thailand. Waiting for Pru to retire so she can accompany me more often."

Marsden forced a smile, then turned to her companions. "I believe you know Todd, our Upper School head, and Arthur Burnham, assistant head?"

"Yes. Hello, gentlemen. Did you know Ms. Parker well?"

Bridgham shook his head, and Burnham looked mildly offended. "We're here representing the school. Shall we go in, Pru? Phil?"

"Here come the Thurberts," she whispered. "She's in last year's Dior. Retirement must be treating them well."

He laughed. "Believe it or not, I know something about the shopping habits of Ms. Thurbert."

Greta stared at him as if he'd sprouted horns.

"A few months ago, Jane was over for dinner, and she told us that Carrie shops at some fancy online consignment site."

"Where'd you think I got this?" Greta asked, running her hands along her waist.

"Come on, Style Queen, time to go in."

As they entered the building, he met the eyes of Lucy Cotter. A tall, robust man in dark navy suit sat beside her. Bill Cotter, he assumed. Gretchen's brother-in-law had been happy to speak with Greta and Stevens, but his knowledge of Harrison's business dealings had been mostly hearsay. Greta described him as a gentleman, very hospitable and kind. Today he looked as if he were waiting to walk the plank.

When all were seated on the straight white benches, Jean Davol, Clerk of the Meeting, rose and welcomed everyone. She read a short poem by May Swenson entitled "Earth Your Dancing Place," which she said had been chosen by Vicky Brown. Then she said, "We are here to celebrate the life of Gretchen Parker. To her friends, family, and all who knew her, let your heart be your guide, if you feel moved to speak. If you do feel moved to speak, we ask that you leave space between speakers for silence. Welcome and God bless."

A long period of silence ensued, punctuated by only a handful of speakers. Claire Rubin spoke briefly about Gretchen as a friend and community member, as did Betty Sue Collins. Shortly after Betty Sue sat down, Suzanna Costa popped up and gave an emotional accounting of her love for Gretchen as "the mother I never had," after which she collapsed against her brother's shoulder, her muffled sobs echoing through the room. Vicky Brown sat on her roommate's other side. Her eyes were filled with tears, yet she appeared uncomfortable and perhaps surprised by Suzanna's tearful display.

*****

Mourners milled about the Commons, plates of appetizers and drinks in hand. Demaris had asked his team to stand at the periphery, observing people's interactions, only intervening or mingling if they saw a need. He, on the other hand, walked slowly through the crowd, stopping briefly to say hello to Bess and her colleagues before moving on. Barry Costa manned the crowded bar, serving beer, wine, and soft drinks, while his sister and two other village women passed platters of appetizers. Suzanna seemed to have recovered and was chatting with people as she passed. Vicky Brown had retreated to a table near the door and was acknowledging people's condolences with weary smiles and offers to join her. Few seemed to be taking her up on her offer.

"May I?" he asked, indicating the empty chair beside her.

"Of course, Lieutenant, please. It was kind of you to come."

"How're you holding up?"

"I'm okay. Just trying to get through this and figure out how to find time to go to Florida and clear out Mother's home."

"Will you sell, then?"

"No, it doesn't belong to me. Mom had life tenancy, but it goes to Greg's kids now. They've been calling daily to see when I can move things out. By the time I get there, they'll have grabbed anything of value, whether it belonged to Mom or not."

"There are legal ways to prevent this."

"It's probably already happened. It's been going on for years. They all have keys. First it was her jewelry, then the silver. Now they'll just grab whatever they can get their hands on. They're vultures. Let 'em have it. The only thing I cared about was Mother."

"Can I assist?"

"Thanks, but no. Suzanna and Barry already offered to fly down either with me or before. I think it's something I'd like to do alone."

"I could call down to the police, I mean."

"Thank you. Let me think about it. I'm going to take three or four personal days and fly down after Marge's service. Poor Marge, such a sweetheart. Do you think it was the same person?"

"Yes."

"I heard about Lee's attack. Do you think the killer is targeting the book club for some reason?"

"I hope not. I think it's more likely that there's another connection."

"Dennis, you mean."

Another book club member, Mary Ann Morgan, receptionist to the village doctor, swooped down, giving Vicky a bear hug. Ordinarily decked out in flamboyant colors and unflattering muumuus, for once she was dressed appropriately in a black pants suit. "Oh, sweetie, how are you?"

Vicky smiled at him over Mary Ann's shoulder as Demaris stood and moved away. As he stepped back into the crowd, he spied Clarice Wills standing alone and moved to her side.

"Hello. How are you?"

"Sad. Gretchen was a dear person."

"A good friend, then?"

She smiled, setting her water glass on a nearby table. "A good patron. She was a frequent visitor, almost every afternoon when she lived in the village."

"Surprised our paths never crossed."

"You were a nooner. She came at tea time, often with a bag of muffins, sandwiches, or scones. I've just now regained my waistline after those teas." She twirled her almost floor-length peasant skirt, matched with a ruffled blouse cinched in at her tiny waist.

"Had you seen her this trip, then?"

"Yes, she came in Tuesday, then again early Wednesday, laden, as always, with those nasty treats from the café."

"How did she seem?"

"Funny you should ask. Tuesday she was her usual jovial self, looking forward to a week of socializing with friends and family, but Wednesday something seemed to be troubling her."

"Did she say what?"

"No. I asked if she was okay. All she said was that after three husbands, she had learned how to take care of herself, and she'd handle this, too."

Might be what got her killed, he mused. At this moment, Becca Rollins joined them, and he gave her a warm smile. "Hello, Becca. Nice to see you."

The teenager nodded before turning to her mother. "Can we *please* go now?"

Clarice gave him an apologetic look before turning to her daughter. "In a little while, Bec. I told you before, you're welcome to walk or wait in the car for me."

"Yeah, right." Becca stalked off, headed for a group that included her father.

"Not the easiest period in her life, Clarice said. "If she doesn't get what she wants from one parent, she goes directly to the other."

They watched as Becca pulled her father's sleeve, drawing him away from a conversation with Arthur Burnham. Garrett did not look pleased, and his response did not appear to be what Becca wanted to hear. She turned away, grabbed a fistful of cheese and crackers, and headed for the side door.

"How's she been the past few days?"

"More angry than usual. She blames herself for Wixie's flight and fright, but I think what happened in the woods scared her, too. Are you any closer to finding out who committed these terrible murders?"

"Wish I could say yes."

"Oh, dear. Here comes Garrett. Will you excuse me, Roger?"

"Of course. Take care."

With a quick glance at his officers' locations, he headed for the side door. The air felt good after the stuffiness within. He spied Becca on a bench overlooking the east side of campus, strolled over, and sat beside her. "Hot in there."

She shrugged.

"Did you know Ms. Parker well?"

"No, Mom dragged me. I only wanted to go to Marge's service, but she made me come to this one, too."

"So, you were close to Ms. Franklin?"

She nodded.

"How so?"

"I helped out in the gallery once or twice, and she was teaching me to paint."

"Oh? Are you planning to major in art at Greenleaf?"

Another shrug. "Maybe. Marge said I had talent."

"Don't know much about Greenleaf's program. I'm a RISD man myself."

Slack-jawed, Becca stared at him. "You paint?"

"Guilty as charged. Haven't we talked about this before?"

"Not that I remember."

"Most of my work stays in my studio, where it probably belongs."

"What d'you do?"

"Oils, some watercolors, some acrylics. Still trying to find my groove. I do a lot of still life, some landscapes, the occasional portrait."

"You any good?"

"As I said, most of my work stays private. I've got a really nice studio at my new house. Once I get settled in and unpacked, I'll let you know. Maybe we can paint together sometime?"

Another shrug.

He spied Pete in the doorway and stood.

"Duty calls, but I'll see you at the Franklin service. I'll also be in touch when the studio's ready for visitors, okay?"

"Okay," she said softly as he turned away.

"Hey, boss," Pete said, "place is starting to thin out, but wanted to let you know that Harrison just arrived, and he appears to be harassing Vicky Brown."

"A little late, isn't he? Come on, let's rescue her."

They spied Dennis Harrison seated beside Vicky Brown, endeavoring to take her hand, which she had withdrawn out of reach. She had turned to Betty Sue, who sat on her other side and was doing her best to ignore him.

"Look at him," Pete said. "He looks like he's auditioning for a part in *Arsenic and Old Lace.*"

Demaris chuckled, but as they neared the table, his expression was stern. "Mr. Harrison, may we have a word?"

"Not now, officers. I have to speak to Vicky."

Demaris gave Pete a look, and with one swift movement Harrison was on his feet and headed to the front door, Stevens on his other side. Once outside, they released him, and for a second it appeared he might collapse in a heap. "How dare you!"

Demaris took several slow, deep breaths. "A little late for this, aren't you?"

"I had a conflict."

"Oh?"

"Not that it's any of your goddamn business, but my wife needed a ride to the airport."

Probably purposely booked her flight at this hour, Demaris thought. "Is she going somewhere?"

"Back to Florida."

"What about you?"

"Well, since you told me I had to stay, I'm trapped, and she didn't want to stay around."

"What time is her flight?"

"Six tonight. She gets nervous and likes to be there really early."

"Providence?"

"Yes, why?"

"Because I would like to speak with her before she departs." He eyed Pete, who stepped away to make a call to the state police.

"Is that really necessary?"

"Won't know until we speak, will we? Now, back to the matter at hand. It was quite clear from Ms. Brown's expression that she did not want to speak with you. Unless you have further business here, I will ask one of my officers to escort you to your car."

"Go to hell," he said, turning away and heading down the hill to the parking lot.

CHAPTER 31

As the last of the mourners departed, the cavernous Commons Hall echoed with the footsteps of the book club ladies and school maintenance crew as they packed away leftovers and cleaned up. Roger walked Bess to the car. "Couple of things to do, but I should be home by seven."

"I'll tackle a few boxes, then heat up some dinner. Is Lois and Cathy's soup okay? We've got lots left. Kind of monotonous, I know, but we'll get into gourmet soon."

"Sounds perfect." He smiled the smile she knew was hers alone and touched her cheek.

He met Greta halfway up the hill as she walked with Vicky Brown and several of Vicky's school colleagues. "Can we drop anyone?" he asked.

"All set," replied a strawberry-blonde twenty something who walked arm and arm with Vicky.

"Vicky, please let us know if you need anything."

"Thank you, Lieutenant." She gave him a wan smile, then followed her friends to a waiting SUV.

"Pete and Brendan are on their way back, boss."

"With Carla Whitmarsh?"

"Yup."

"Good. Anyone still in the Commons?"

"Only the cleanup crew. The last of the book club ladies just left, as did Suzanna and Barry Costa."

"Okay, let's go."

*****

They had just enough time to grab waters and sit before the guest house door opened and Carla Harrison stalked in, followed by Pete and Stevens. Dark brown eyes blazing, she advanced toward Demaris. "Are you in charge here?"

"Yes. Roger Demaris, Regional Homicide Division. We're investigating the murders of Gretchen Parker and Margery Franklin."

"So I've been told by your little mod squad. How dare you prevent me from flying home?"

Harrison's wife looked to be half her husband's age, petite, stylish, and well put together. Her short dark hair cut on an angle defined a delicate, pale face. Not much over five feet, she wore heather-gray slacks, pale blue silk blouse, and a thin gold necklace, a gray jacket flung over one shoulder.

"I'm sorry for the inconvenience. We will fix things with the airlines so you will be issued a new ticket at no charge."

"That doesn't fix the appointments I'll have to cancel for tomorrow and the incredible inconvenience of staying another night in this backwater hellhole. Rest assured, I will be taking this up with my attorney."

"This is a homicide investigation, not a garden party, Ms. Harrison."

"The name is Whitmarsh. Now, what the hell do you want?"

"Can you tell us where you were Wednesday morning? Were you with your husband?"

"No, I was headed to Wellesley to visit my sister, where I remained until late last night. I should have changed my ticket and flown out of Boston."

"Can anyone verify your departure time?"

"You cannot believe I had anything to do with the death of these women?"

"They were both former lovers of your husband."

"Yes, about a gazillion years ago. I didn't even know them. Ran into Gretchen Parker a few times with Dennis. Always very awkward. And I wouldn't know the Franklin woman if I fell over her."

"Have you ever visited her gallery in Mattapoisett?"

She paused, staring at him. "Well, yes, as a matter of fact. I've actually bought several pieces, not by Franklin. I collect Palla Forest's work."

"Oh?"

"Palla and I are old friends."

"I see. So in all your visits to purchase art, you never met the gallery owner?"

"Never. Always dealt with that bobble-headed assistant of hers, Cathy or Katie."

"Carol Martin?"

"That's the one."

"If you and Palla are such great friends, why not purchase her work directly?"

"I do both, but sometimes she slips a piece into the gallery before I've seen it, and then I have no choice."

"I see. So, getting back to Wednesday morning."

"I left the condo at around ten-thirty and stopped for coffee on my way out of town. Then I was off. Arrived in Wellesley at noon. You can check with my sister if you like."

"Thank you. My detectives will take down her information. Was your husband still at home when you left?"

"Of course. If he's not playing golf, Dennis rarely gets up before eleven."

"Well, thank you, Ms. Whitmarsh. I'm going to have to ask you to stay in Old Harbor for at least a day or so. Will that be a problem?"

"Do I have a choice?"

"Thanks so much for your flexibility. Officer Stevens will drive you home."

"Whoopee! Just where I want to be." She grabbed her enormous black purse and stomped out.

Pete stared at the door that had just been slammed in their faces. "Well, that was fun."

"Get some rest, you two. Tomorrow, we hammer away at the Harrison kids and Dennis's and Carla's alibis. I also want corroboration from someone besides Steele Rubin and Carol Martin about their time together on Wednesday and Thursday. Something about it seems off."

"I found something interesting today, boss," Greta said, shuffling papers as she watched the two men.

"Oh?"

"Palla Forest had a fling with Dennis Harrison."

Pete grabbed a beer from the refrigerator and plopped down on the sofa. "Jesus Christ, I'm so sick of this guy! He's not handsome, and his personality sucks. Palla Forest's not my type, but she's gorgeous and young enough to be his granddaughter."

Demaris shook his head. "Wonder he has time to sleep. How'd you hear about this fling, and when did it happen?"

"When she was in high school. Overheard Garrett Rollins telling a group of his colleagues. As you know, there's no love lost between him and Palla at the moment. They were talking about Wixie's disappearance and how horrible Palla's been to Becca since then."

"I shouldn't think they interact much."

"Apparently, there was some kind of kerfuffle this morning, when Palla came to pick up Wixie. For once, Wixie wanted to stay at her dad's. Seems Palla's been on a painting frenzy and very short-tempered lately."

"Pete, I just realized, I don't have my car," Demaris said. "Will you run me home? I'd like to stop by campus on the way, see if we can locate Rollins. We can run Palla Forest down tomorrow."

Pete hopped up, pouring three quarters of his beer down the kitchen sink. "Sure, boss."

*****

After finding no one home in the dorm, the two men walked over to the dining hall, where they spied Rollins busing his tray of half-eaten food to the wash-up area. Joan Nettleman walked beside him, chattering away as usual. She spotted them before he did. "Uh, oh, Garr—it's the police. What have we done now?"

Absently, Demaris wondered if Joan were flirting with Rollins. If yes, he didn't give her favorable odds. "Hello, sorry to intrude. Might we have a brief word, Mr. Rollins?"

Joan frowned. "Well, I know when I'm not wanted. See you back at the dorm, Garr."

"Actually, Joan, I wonder if we couldn't have a quick word after we speak to Garrett?"

She regarded him curiously, then said, "I'll get coffee and wait over there, but I have to be in the studio in twenty-five minutes." The rotund, flamboyantly garbed art teacher trundled off to the other side of the room.

"Thanks. We won't be long."

Rollins set down his tray and followed them to an empty table at the far end of the room. Pete sat to the side, silent as always, as Demaris asked, "Do you and Joan live in the same dorm, then?"

"Yup, she's on the girls' side. It's kind of like a duplex. Each side has three floors, but never the twain shall meet. The apartments are adjacent. They open onto the same back hallway, unfortunately for me."

"Oh?"

"Joan used to live in another dorm, but after Palla and I split up and I moved back to campus, she somehow persuaded Kevin LeBlanc to switch apartments. Kevin's another casualty of divorce and seems totally indifferent to where he lives."

"Why would Joan move next to you?" Demaris asked, knowing the answer.

"Apparently our Joanie has developed a crush on me. I mean, I love Joan. She's a character and she has a heart of gold, but her and me? Never gonna happen. What did you want to see me about?"

"Detective Burke overheard you talking after the funeral about a relationship between Ms. Gardner and Dennis Harrison."

"Didn't know you guys would be eavesdropping at a funeral."

"Is it true?"

"Yes, the lech seduced her in high school. Palla was fifteen, for Christ's sake. She played softball with Harrison's oldest granddaughter, Maisie. Not even sure how it happened, but with that old goat, it doesn't take much."

Pot calling the kettle black, Demaris thought, studying Rollins. "I wouldn't have thought Harrison's grandchildren were that old."

"Maisie was born when Dennis Junior was still in high school. He married the mother, Ruth. They're still married, as far as I know. Mindy and Steele Rubin kept the kid while Mommy and Daddy went to college. When Ruth graduated from Wheaton, she took over full-time parenting while Dennis Junior got his doctorate. They lived with the Rubins until he got the job at Greenleaf."

"Where's Maisie now?"

"Not sure. Dennis and Ruth had a couple more kids, I think, but they haven't lived in the area for at least ten years. Even then, they lived in Mattapoisett, not here. Maisie went to Moses Brown, then away, so I never saw her unless at an athletic event. The athletic teams are mostly tri-town, except for soccer, 'cause the towns are so small."

"So, before you informed people yesterday, did anyone besides you know about Dennis and Palla?"

"Jesus Christ, I'm not that much of a bastard. Palla and I may be at odds right now, but I'd never betray her secret. No, Suzanna Costa brought it up. She told Joan and that was it. The whole village'll know before the week's out."

"Did Joan say why Suzanna raised the subject?"

"No, only said they bumped into each other in town yesterday, and they were talking about the murders and how horrible they were. Naturally, the subject of Dennis Harrison came up, and Suzanna said something, and Joan said something, and I was mentioned, and blah, blah. Suzanna said something like, 'Garrett must have been shocked to learn about Palla and Dennis,' and that was it. Like a dog with a bone, Joan gnawed and chewed till she had every last detail. I was trying to tone it down today, actually. It'll bother Palla that people know about this."

"How would Suzanna know about this, do you think?"

"They're about the same age, and Suzanna played softball. Maybe she noticed something at the time."

"Thanks, Rollins. When we speak to Joan, we'll ask her not to spread this around. Who else was in the group today?"

"Kitty Bigalow, Bess, and Jane. None of them are too gossipy, except Kitty, sometimes. Marriage to a minister's a bit boring, I imagine."

*****

They sat opposite Joan Nettleman at a round table at the quiet end of the cafeteria. "Thanks for waiting," Demaris said.

"No problem. What can I do for you?"

"Bess mentioned that you have questions about the originality of some of Palla Forest's work?"

"That witch? Palla, I mean, not Bess. She's strictly a hacker. Couldn't paint her way out of a paper bag if she wasn't copying the work of others."

"Like?"

"Most of her early works are exact copies of paintings by Jan Weitmar, a lesser-known Belgian artist. All she did was add a touch or two of New England to copies of his landscapes. Look him up. You'll see."

"That's not strictly illegal, is it?"

"No, she's not forging anything, but she sure ain't creating anything new, either."

"She sells well."

"Yes, she does. And if I step off my bitchy soapbox, I have to admit that I've carried a grudge since she and I were members of a painting group. I had to drop out because they started meeting during the day, but I would have anyway. We had a show and Palla was in charge. Everyone else had one painting entered and she had half a dozen, all of which sold at high prices."

"I've seen your work. It's quite original," he said.

"Now you're being kind. I think the word you're looking for is *wacky*. Don't look so surprised. I know what people say."

"I wonder if we might ask that you keep the gossip about Palla Forest and Dennis Harrison to yourself? I've asked Garrett to speak to Kitty and the others."

She blanched. "Of course."

"Well, thanks, Joan."

"No problem. When are you going to invite me out to your fancy new studio? I hear your paintings are pretty damn good."

He smiled, standing up. "No doubt from my completely biased wife. Not sure my work is ready for the real world, but you would be welcome anytime. Bess and I have been saying we should have a dinner party, once all the boxes disappear. Take care."

*****

As he and Bess sat watching the sunset, sipping an excellent Pinot Noir, she sighed. "How will this village recover from so much darkness?"

"Time, my darling," he said, closing his eyes, wanting to forget the case for a few hours.

Bess had confirmed Rollins's account of the afternoon's conversation and had then called Kitty and Jane, who both said they had not mentioned the revelation of Palla and Dennis to anyone, and would not. Time to let go, hold his beloved's hand, and let night fall around them.

CHAPTER 32

"The Whitmarsh woman's timeline checks out," Pete said as he took a seat beside Greta, the remains of another huge Tilly's breakfast all around them.

"Where are we with her husband?"

Stevens set down his coffee and grabbed his notebook. "As he told us, he was home in his condo Wednesday morning. Went out for a drink with an old golfing buddy, but that wasn't until late afternoon."

"He's a bit of a lounge lizard in addition to being an old goat," Pete added, leaning back in his chair.

"Careful, these chairs are old," Demaris said. "What about Thursday afternoon, Brendan?"

"Some gaps, but people did see him here and there, running errands in the village."

"Okay, well, Pete and I are headed over to Greenleaf this morning. Dennis Junior's agreed to see us at eleven and his sister, Lena, is joining us. By happy coincidence, they'd planned to have lunch today. You all set with the brother?"

"Yes, sir, Brendan and I are meeting Steele Harrison at one of his jobs. He said if we hang around, he'll have time to talk with us before he goes to the next property."

"Okay, then, good luck. Pete, let's go."

"But it only takes a little over an hour to get to Greenleaf, boss. We'll be way early."

"I have a stop to make first. Bring the car around. I'll be out in a minute."

"But?"

Demaris cleared his throat and gazed up over his glasses at his second-in-command as Greta gazed from one man to the other waiting for an explosion.

Pete raised his hands. "Okay, okay, big secret. You coming?"

"In a minute."

As soon as the door closed behind Dugan, their boss laughed. "He's such a pain in the ass, so I like to keep him guessing once in a while. I want to stop off at the Forest woman's studio, that's all."

Greta chuckled. "You're wicked, boss. Poor Pete."

*****

By the time they pulled into the dirt driveway alongside the barn Palla Forest used as studio, Dugan's face was no longer red, and his shoulders had relaxed. Demaris gazed at him. "Sorry, buddy."

Silence.

"I'm not sure but this wouldn't go better with just me."

"Whatever you say."

For several minutes, he stared at the young man who was as much a son to him as his Owen, then said, "Fuck the woman. Come on, partner."

As they neared the barn door, they heard the woman herself screaming. "I have a deadline! What's the matter with you people?"

Pete knocked and she yelled, "Now what?"

The door creaked as it swung open. Palla Forest held her cell phone, gesturing in the air as she listened. When she spied the two men, she scowled and turned her back. "Listen, Ted, I have to go. I want those paints today, do you understand me? Fine, well, fuck you, too!" She clicked off and turned to face them.

"Bad time?" Demaris asked.

"What d'you want?"

"Just a few minutes. Okay to speak here?" he said.

"No, it is not. I never entertain anyone in here. Come on." She led the way out the back door to the walkway leading to her house. They stepped into a small light-filled kitchen, new by the look of it, with white marble counter tops and warm wood floors. White cabinets, many of them glass-fronted, held brightly colored pottery and glassware. Copper pots and pans hung above them, freshly polished.

"Nice kitchen," Pete said, thinking about the tiny galley in his condo.

"Yes, the only contribution my soon-to-be ex-husband ever made to our marriage."

"And Wixie?" Demaris asked.

"Well, duh? Of course, Wixie. If she didn't love him so much, I'd move away from here."

"Isn't this where your reputation as an artist resides?"

"Perhaps, but I'm flexible. That wouldn't be a problem. Now, what are you here about? I'm swamped and need to get back to work."

"Something came to light about your past, Ms. Forest. We just wanted to check its veracity."

"Oh?"

"It's about your relationship with Dennis Harrison."

Her face turned pale, and Palla Forest gasped. "Oh, my, God, Garrett can be a bastard, but I never thought he would stoop so low."

"Your husband was not the source."

"Oh?"

"Is it true?"

"Unfortunately, yes. So if not Garrett, who told you?"

"Suzanna Costa."

She shook her head. "I didn't know she knew. After all these years, she's never said a thing. Why was she telling people now?"

"It came up in conversation about the murders, with a third party."

"Does the whole village know?"

"I believe we've successfully shut down the rumor mill. I don't believe it will go any farther."

All the fight knocked out of her, Forest sunk into a chair, tears rimming her eyes. "Doesn't matter. What do I care? Wasn't a big deal. Not much more than a one-night stand anyway. Just sucks that I lost my virginity to that bastard."

"I'm sorry."

"Don't be. Years of therapy have cured me of Dennis Harrison."

"Why don't I believe you?"

She shrugged.

"How did it end?"

"As I said, it wasn't much, and Dennis moved on to someone else, I'm sure."

"So, he never approached you again?"

She shook her head. "I got the feeling someone had warned him off."

"Oh, any idea who?"

"No, but the next few times I saw him, he almost seemed scared to approach me."

"Has he made overtures since then?"

"Never. After our pathetic affair, I've probably seen the man three times. He stopped coming to Maisie's softball games. That's how we met."

"Yes."

"He's a predator."

"Yes."

"Do you think he's responsible for the murders?"

"We don't know, but he does keep coming up."

"That's because that asshole has slept with over half the women within fifty miles. Not that he's in the same class, but he gives Warren Beatty a run for his money. What was he, a thousand women in as many days?"

Demaris smiled. "I believe it was a bit more, but fortunately Ms. Benning has tamed him at last."

"Unlike Carla Whitmarsh, poor woman."

"You're friends, I understand."

"She collects my work, so yes, we've become friendly. And she knows nothing about Dennis and me. I'd like to keep it that way."

"Of course. I wanted to ask you one other delicate question."

"Oh, God, what now?"

"How did you develop your particular style as a painter?"

"Excuse me?"

"Someone recently hinted that some of your work might be derivative, even copies of the work of others?"

"How dare you! Who is spreading such lies?"

"I believe there's a little-known Belgian painter, Jan Weitmar, whose work bears a striking resemblance to yours, especially his landscapes?"

"Never heard of him. Now if that's all, I've got work to do."

"Of course. How's Wixie doing?"

"Fine. This week her father walks on water, so she throws a tantrum if I try to bring her home."

"Is that so bad, with you so busy?"

"No, actually. I've given in and am letting her stay, at least until this crunch is over."

"Take care, Ms. Forest."

"Good-bye."

CHAPTER 33

They took back roads most of the way to the college town of Greenleaf, which was sixty miles northwest of Old Harbor. On this warm fall day, the leaves had begun to change color, oranges and reds sprinkled amongst the green of the woods lining both sides of the road.

Brother and sister were waiting in his office when they arrived. Dennis rose and came to shake their hands, while his sister stayed seated.

Dennis Harrison Junior was slender and pale with features so handsome that one might call him beautiful. His straight dirty-blond hair fell over his eyes, and he combed it back with one hand as he shook hands with the other. Demaris suspected the hair thing happened hundreds of times throughout the professor's day. The young women must love him, he mused, taking a seat opposite their host. Pete sat in a chair by the door.

Unlike her brother, Lena Harrison was her father's daughter, her ruddy cheeks so like his, eyes the same languid green, almost muddy. Short and full around the middle, she wore white leggings, black ballet slippers, and a long, full tunic in a fabric of bold multicolored geometric shapes. He wondered if the tunic was one of her designs.

Dennis cleared his throat and combed back his hair. "So, Lieutenant, you wanted to see us? Can I get you anything? Water? Coffee? Juice?"

"Thank you. We're fine. Yes, we wanted to ask you about your parents and your knowledge of the two women murdered in our area this past week. I'm assuming you've heard about Gretchen Parker and Margery Franklin?"

"Yes, my father called. And in case you're wondering, when I say 'my father,' I'm referring to Steele Rubin, the man who raised us. In fact, the only father we've known."

"So, he phoned both of you?"

Dennis leaned forward to pat his sister's hand. "Just me. Lenie's been out of town. When she got back, I told her."

"Oh. Where were you traveling, Ms. Harrison?"

"I was on a buying trip in New York."

"So were you away all last week?"

"Yes, until Friday evening. My husband picked me up at the train at around eight-thirty."

"How about you, Mr. Harrison? Where were you last Wednesday and Thursday?"

"Hold on. You can't think we had anything to do with these women's deaths? We hardly knew them," he said.

"Ms. Parker was married to your father, your biological father, and was good friends with your stepmother, as was Marge Franklin."

Lena sat up straight and stared daggers at Demaris. "My dear sir, we see Dennis Harrison once a year, if that, and that woman never came to our happy little gatherings, I can assure you."

"So you never saw her?"

"I didn't say never. Sometimes I'd see her in Mattapoisett. I stay with my dad quite a lot, especially during the summer."

"What about Ms. Franklin?"

"Sometimes I'd wander into her rinky-dink gallery. She carried a few decent artists—Palla Forest, for one."

"You appreciate Ms. Forest's work, then?"

"It's okay."

"Listen, Lieutenant," said Dennis, "I'd love to linger and chat about art, but I have office hours in fifteen minutes. I was here all day Wednesday and Thursday."

"Teaching?"

"My teaching days are Mondays and Wednesdays. When I wasn't in class, I had office hours and a few meetings. The rest of the time I was attempting to get out from under a mountain of papers that need grading. It's the third week of the semester, and I'm already buried."

"Did you resent Gretchen Parker for marrying your father?"

"As I said, we do not think of Dennis Harrison as our father. Once our mother died, we washed our hands of the man. Only see him once a year for his pathetic dinners so he doesn't keep phoning and pestering us. But, to answer your question, no, I didn't resent Mrs. Parker. I barely knew her and didn't care to know her."

"Can anyone verify seeing you buried in your paperwork?"

"That's enough," he said, rising from his chair. "Our father warned us about you. My sister and I know nothing about these women's deaths, barely knew them, and thus have absolutely nothing to contribute to your inquiry. If you have any further questions, please see my father's attorney. He will be arranging any future meetings. Now, if you'll excuse us, I have office hours, and Lena has to be on her way."

"Very generous of Mr. Rubin to bankroll your legal affairs." Demaris knew he was baiting Harrison, but he decided to push, to see if he took after his adoptive father.

"Go to hell. We've tried to be civil, and this is what we get. Get the hell out and take your underling and his notepad with you."

Demaris stood and stared from brother to sister. After several deep breaths, he spoke softly. "It's Detective Dugan to you, Professor Harrison. If you want to insult someone, I would find a mirror. We will, indeed, ask Mr. Rubin's attorney to arrange something, should we need to speak again, but I doubt that will be necessary after we make inquiries on campus and in your neighborhood concerning your activities last week. Once we've completed our canvas, your involvement in this matter will be superfluous."

"Now, wait a minute!"

"Good-bye, Professor, Ms. Harrison." He followed Pete out of the office and closed the door.

As they neared the car, Pete said, "Are we really gonna scour the campus?"

His boss chuckled. "No, he pissed me off. My gut tells me those two aren't involved, but I couldn't resist tryin' to get a rise out of the asshole. I actually meant what I said. If we need to come back, we will, but I think they're telling the truth. Their stepfather is another matter. Let's head back and see if Greta and Stevens learned anything from sibling number three."

*****

"Not much, boss," was Greta's answer when he asked about their conversation with Steele Harrison. "Nice guy, straight-shooter, laid back. Didn't have much good to say about his biological father, or his siblings, for that matter."

"I like him already," Pete said.

Greta looked from one to the other, a puzzled look on her face.

"Let's just say that Pete and I don't have much good to say about the other two siblings. Fortunately, I'm pretty sure they're not involved, so we won't need to see them again."

"Steele did say that his stepfather was good to them, but not all that good to his wives, either of them. His marriage—Steele Harrison's, I mean—seems happy."

Demaris nodded. "Not surprised. Lizzy's a sweetheart, or at least, that's what Bess tells me. She's always been pleasant enough when I've run into her at school things. Come to think of it, the few times I've seen Lizzy, I don't recall her husband being with her."

"He told us he never socializes, except an occasional evening with family. Says he's an introvert and his wife is very understanding."

"Brendan, your technological wizardry reveal anything new today?"

Stevens smiled and grabbed his notes. "Pete told me to check into Barry Costa's prison record. He doesn't have one that I could find, but he did do a stint in juvie when he was sixteen. Records are sealed, but I managed to find someone who remembered the case. Theft and breaking and entering. He and a couple of his buddies were breaking into fancy summer houses over at the Bluffs. Made quite a profit, apparently. He was held at the Wilson Juvenile Facility. Sentence was two years, but he flipped out after a week and was transferred to a psychiatric facility, where he served out his sentence. According to the guys I talked to, Costa has severe claustrophobia."

Demaris knew better than to ask the young officer about the source of his information about Barry Costa. His youngest officer had an uncanny ability to uncover information, which often proved invaluable, even if occasionally obtained from dubious sources. "Thanks, Brendan. I doubt the tattoos are from juvie, but their origin may have to remain a mystery."

"We could always ask him," Pete said.

Demaris's phone rang. It was Chief Smith. "Hey, Roger, thought you'd wanta know. Bob Franklin's awake. He's a bit foggy, but the doctor says he should be fine in a day or two. They're going ahead with the funeral Thursday. Franklin's going home this afternoon with his daughter taking care of him."

"Isn't that a bit soon?"

"Apparently Franklin insisted. Says he wants to be home tomorrow to sort through some things. If he's not better, he'll go back."

"Think he'd be up to a visitor?"

"I'd check with his daughter once they're home."

CHAPTER 34

"He's pretty groggy, sir," Rosemary said as she opened the door. "Says he wants to see you, but I wouldn't stay too long."

"Of course." Demaris and Pete followed Franklin's daughter into the living room, where her father sat in his recliner, watching a football game. When he spied them, he clicked off the TV with the remote.

"Hello, Mr. Franklin. I'm Lieutenant Demaris, and this is Detective Dugan. We're terribly sorry for your loss. Your wife was a lovely person."

"Yes, she was," he said. Tears rimmed his bloodshot eyes.

"How are you feeling?"

"Like I was hit over the head with a baseball bat. Things are still a bit fuzzy, but doc says each day will be better."

"Can you think of anyone who might want to harm your wife?"

"No, no one. Everyone loved Margie."

"I understand she got together last week with the other victim, Gretchen Parker?"

"Did they? Don't remember."

"Dad, Gretchen ate dinner with you and mom. Last Tuesday? Here at the house? You had lobster?"

"Did we? Gee, I don't remember, sweetie. Last I remember seeing Gretch was about six months ago when she was up."

Rosemary turned Demaris. "This is where he's fuzzy. Doesn't remember anything from the recent past. Nothing about the accident on the boat or what he did last week. The doctor says it's very common and his memory will probably come back gradually."

"So, he had dinner with the ladies, then?"

"Yes. When I came home from work, they were on the deck, chatting."

"Mr. Franklin, what about Ms. Parker? You've known her for a while now. Can you think of anyone with a grudge against her?"

He shrugged. "She was Margie's friend. Knew who she was on account of we've both lived around here for many years, but until I married Margie three years ago, I only knew Gretchen by reputation."

"And what was that?"

"Excuse me?"

"Ms. Parker's reputation?"

"Only that she was a local gal who had had the misfortune to marry that bastard Dennis Harrison."

Rosemary paled and started to tremble.

Demaris gazed over at her. "Are you alright, Rosemary?"

"Yes. No. I'm just afraid father's going to excite himself and land back in the hospital."

Demaris reached out and patted her hand. "Not to worry. We're done here, and your father can rest. If either of you think of anything, please don't hesitate to call any one of us." He handed her a card, which she took with shaking hands.

"Take care, Mr. Franklin. If we don't see you before, we'll see you at Mrs. Franklin's service."

Franklin nodded and mumbled, "Of course," never taking his eyes from his daughter.

As they drove back to Old Harbor, Pete asked, "What was all that about?"

"What it's always been about. Dennis Harrison. I want to know if he ever had anything to do with Rosemary Franklin or her mother. Something frightened that girl, and it wasn't her father's state of health."

*****

Tuesday afternoon, Bess left school and went into town. After returning her library books, she headed for the fish market. As she opened the door, Rosemary Franklin stepped out. "Rosemary, hello. I heard your father's home. How's he doing?"

"Pretty well. Memory of the past few weeks hasn't come back, and he's still got a nasty headache."

"I'll bet he does. Do you two need anything? I could make you a meal and bring it over tomorrow?"

"Thanks, but we're great. The book club ladies have brought enough food to keep us for a month. And they're organizing all the food after Marge's service, which is incredibly generous of them."

"Small-town people have their highs and lows, but when someone's in need, they are always there. Let me know once you dig out from under all that food."

"Well, well, haven't seen you in a while." As an unfamiliar male voice spoke behind Bess, she watched the color drain from Rosemary's face, eyes registering what looked like fear.

Bess turned around. The man looked vaguely familiar, but she couldn't place him.

"Aren't you going to introduce us, Rosie?"

"Bess, this is Barry Costa," she stammered, eyes downcast, hands trembling.

"Oh, yes, you tended bar at Sunday's reception after Ms. Parker's service. Bess Demaris." Bess extended her hand, which he grasped with limp, sweaty indifference.

"The cop's wife. Hey, nice to meet you."

"Bess, I've got to go. Dad's waitin' on me."

"Of course. Take care, Rosemary."

"Hey, Rosie, wait up. How's your dad?"

Before he could follow the frightened young woman, Bess surprised herself by grabbing hold of his sleeve. "That's enough, Mr. Costa. She clearly doesn't want to talk right now. We had best leave her alone."

His dark, beady eyes flashed fire as he pulled away from her grasp. "Not that it's any of your business."

"Excuse me?"

"Your hubby may be a cop, but you really don't want to mess with me."

"Are you threatening me, Mr. Costa?"

He laughed. "Just jokin' with ya. No one in this town can take a joke."

Without another word, she pushed by him and headed into the fish market.

Al Roberts, the fishmonger, took one look at her and said, "Hey, Bess, you okay? You look a little green around the gills."

"I'm fine, Al. Just had an unpleasant encounter."

"With Barry Costa. I saw you through the window. Don't let that punk rattle you. First-class jerk. Sorry to see him around town again. Hope it's only temporary. What'll you have?"

"Two of those lovely salmon filets. Thanks, Al."

*****

Demaris walked into Village Books alone. He had left Pete with Greta and Stevens. The three were enjoying one of Tilly's enormous lunches. He had eaten a half sandwich, then excused himself.

He spied the owner on a stool at the rear of the shop. "Hey, Clary."

She gave him a warm smile. "Thanks for coming. Coffee?"

"No, thanks."

She motioned to the sitting area in the left alcove, his favorite spot. "So you two are finally together?"

"Didn't we already talk about this?"

"Yes, but you can't blame a girl for being be heartbroken."

"Clary, is this isn't why you wanted to see me, is it?"

"No, but you looked so incredibly sexy walking in here that I couldn't help myself."

"What is it, Clary?"

"I'm worried about Becca. She's scared about something, but she won't tell me what. Now she's insisted on going to Marge Franklin's service and she barely knew the woman. I mean, Marge had started giving her painting lessons, but they'd only had a couple."

"Has she confided in her father, perhaps?"

"Not that I know of. Garrett and I are not the greatest communicators."

"What do you want from me? If she's not talking to you, I doubt she'll open up to me. I could talk to Garrett if you like."

"Thank you, Roger. I'd be grateful. And I'm happy for you and Bess. Really, I am. She's a lucky woman."

"And I am the luckiest of men."

"Yes," she said, quietly as she rose and kissed his cheek.

*****

Later, over dinner, Bess debated, then told her husband about the encounter with Barry Costa. Her revelation elicited the reaction she had expected. He exploded, swearing under his breath. "I'll kill the bastard."

"No, you won't. It was harmless. He's just a weasely little man."

"Nonetheless, Pete and I will have a word with the weasel tomorrow."

"It's really not necessary, darling." She could see that he was breathing mindfully, slowly calming down.

"How was Rosemary?

"Fine, until Barry Costa showed up. She was clearly uncomfortable, almost seemed scared of him."

"He's a bully."

"Still, this seemed more personal, something between the two of them."

CHAPTER 35

"I'll be off, then," Bess said. She had an early morning breakfast meeting with her department.

"Have a good day, my love."

"You, too. There's Pete pulling in now."

"I wish we were still in the Berkshires."

"Me, too." He kissed her softly, and she disappeared as Pete stepped in. "Morning, boss."

"Want coffee?" he asked.

"Thanks, but I stopped at the café on my way here. Got you one, too."

"Let's roll, then."

"Where to?"

"The Glen."

"Yeah?"

"I want to speak to Barry Costa. Then we'll head over to the guest house. Are Greta and Brendan there?"

"Yup, still checking on Steele Rubin's story."

*****

Suzanna Costa met them in the condo parking lot. "Good morning, Lieutenant. Did you need to see us? Vicky's already left for school, and I'm late."

"It's actually your brother we want to talk to. Is he in?" Demaris watched her expression change from open to guarded.

"Why?"

"Just a few questions. You go along. We don't want to keep you."

Reluctantly, she turned and headed to her car. "Good luck. He's a heavy sleeper and doesn't like to get up early," she called over her shoulder.

Pete knocked for almost ten minutes before a disheveled visage opened the door in a tee shirt and boxers. "What the hell? Did you forget your key?" he asked, obviously expecting his sister.

"Good morning, Mr. Costa. May we have a word?" Pete pushed into the condo, followed by his boss.

"This isn't a great time. As you can see, I've just woken up."

"We'll wait, if you'd like to dress," Demaris said quietly.

Costa stared from one to the other, then shrugged. "Suit yourself. I'll be right out."

When he reappeared, he had pulled on jeans. "So? Want coffee?"

"No, thanks," Demaris said.

"Well, I do. Hold on." He disappeared into the kitchen and reappeared a minute later with large mug of coffee. He plopped on the sofa and indicated other chairs surrounding it. "So, what's this about?"

"How's Vicky holding up?"

"Okay, I guess. I'm back and forth from here to friends in Northport, so I don't see her much."

"Did you know her mother well?"

"Not like Suzie did. I left town before Vick and Suz got tight in high school."

"So you didn't know Ms. Parker and Vicky growing up?"

"Nope. I'm seven years older than my sister and, as I said, Vick and Suz weren't friendly before high school."

"What about Rosemary Franklin?"

If the question surprised him, Costa's face didn't show it. "Again, much younger than me. Different crowd. Oh, I know what this is about. Your wife told you we met yesterday."

"Yes, she did. She also said that your presence seemed upsetting to Ms. Franklin."

"Oh? Can't imagine why."

"I'll ask you again. How well do you know Ms. Franklin?"

"Not well at all. She was a little kid when I left town. Used to follow me around like a puppy. Had a bit of a crush on me, I think."

"Then I should think she would be glad to see you instead of frightened."

"Look, Lieutenant, I don't know what the hell you heard, but I saw Rosie, said hello, and went on my way. Your nosy wife was the one who pushed the conversation."

Pete stood. "Now wait a minute, you."

Demaris placed a hand on his assistant's knee. His eyes flashed fire, but his voice remained calm. "You will refrain from harassing Rosemary Franklin, and if you ever go near my wife again, I'll have you arrested. Are we clear?"

"On what charge?"

"Harassment."

"Jesus Christ, we met on the street. It's a free country."

"Not for you, it isn't."

"Look Demaris, I know about you. I grew up here, remember? I know my rights. Now, if there's nothing further, get the hell out and take your bulldog with you."

"Listen, you asshole." Pete's face was beet red.

Demaris watched their host smirk at the reaction he had provoked.

"That's enough, Pete. Let's go. Remember, Costa, stay away from them."

As they reached the car, the bright red flush began to fade from Pete's cheeks. "I could have beaten that twit to a pulp."

Demaris chuckled. "I'm sure you could have, but he's not worth it. Come on. And if you run into him around the condos, walk away, *comprende?*"

*****

They found Greta and Stevens at their computers, remnants of breakfast still on the table. After asking Stevens to clean up and bus the dishes over to Tilly, Demaris waited until all four were seated.

"Anything new?"

"From what we've found, I can't imagine Claire Rubin's kids had any problem with Gretchen Parker or Marge Franklin," Greta said. "They barely know Dennis Harrison's kids. I get the impression that they're not close and that their visits to the Rubins are planned so the two families don't overlap."

"Where's Harrison now? Did you check in with him yesterday?"

"Yes, and his wife, Carla 'I have nothing to contribute to this mess,' are very irritated not to be in Florida."

"Too bad. I want everything you two can dig up on Barry Costa. He's a cocky bastard, and even if he hasn't been in jail since juvie, I can't believe he isn't wanted for something. Probably has a dozen aliases."

A knock at the door interrupted them, and they were surprised to see Dennis Harrison.

"Mr. Harrison, to what do we owe this pleasure?" Demaris asked.

Harrison took a seat at the table facing him. "I certainly hope so. I've got a wife who's ready to kill me, and two of my three children are right behind her."

"I'm sorry to hear they're upset, but this is a murder investigation. And every time we turn around, we run into you. If your family members have complaints, feel free to refer them to me. You have my contact information, I believe?"

"Listen, I know I've led a dissolute life and pretty much screwed everyone close to me, but I'm not a killer and neither are any of my family. I put my kids through hell. This isn't fair to them."

"It's not fair to Gretchen Parker or Margery Franklin, either."

"I don't suppose Carla could head home?"

"Let's give it a day or two and see where we are."

Defeated and weary, Harrison stood. "That's easy for you to say. You don't have to go home to my house."

"Good luck, and do than Ms. Whitmarsh for her patience."

"Yeah, right. I value my neck too much."

"That's an odd choice of words, given the manner of the past week's murders."

"Give me break, will you? That's all I'm asking." As he closed the door, Greta stepped in from the bedroom, where she had excused herself to make a call.

"I just talked to Rosemary Franklin. Her dad's napping now, but he feels better and wants to see you. She said around three would work for them."

*****

Franklin greeted them at the door. "Thanks for accommodating the nap schedule. I seem to need lots of 'em now. Come in. Rosie is off doing errands, but I can get you something to drink, if you like."

"We're fine, thank you," Demaris said.

"My daughter's my keeper right now, I'm 'fraid. Doesn't like to leave me alone, but she went 'cause you guys were comin'. Sit, please." He took the recliner, and Pete and Demaris sat on the sofa beside him.

"Everything all set for the service tomorrow?"

"Yes, her friends have been very helpful. Not sure what we'd have done without them."

"Do you and Rosemary need transportation? My team and I will all be attending and would be happy to drive you both."

"Thanks, but the funeral home will collect us."

"How are you feeling?"

"Much better, even though my memory of the last few weeks is still not back."

"No thought on who might want to harm your wife?"

"No, as I told you the other day, everyone loved Margie. She was a wonderful wife, stepmom, and friend. I s'pose she could've pissed off someone at the gallery—maybe some schlocky artist she refused to hang—but not that I heard. Let's face it, no one kills over artwork, do they?"

"You'd be surprised. I do have one question about your daughter. My wife, Bess, saw her in town the other day. While they were talking, Barry Costa came along. Bess got the impression that his appearance upset Rosemary."

Franklin's face clouded over, his eyes full of fury. "That bastard. I told him not to come within a mile of Rosie. How dare he speak to her."

"Did something happen between them?"

"Rape, that's what happened."

"Was he arrested?"

"No, claimed it was consensual. Happened when she was fourteen. He claimed they were dating. Rosemary was just a kid, flattered by the attentions of an older guy. He's an evil bastard, Lieutenant. Preyed on my baby, took away her innocence, and broke her heart. I hired a private detective, who followed him around. He was seeing a couple of other women besides Rosie. Not sure who they were.

"I confronted Costa and told him I was going to press charges, so he skipped town. Hadn't seen or heard anything about him until two or three weeks ago when Marge saw him in town. Even though we weren't married at the time, I'd told her what had happened with Rosie. She knew I'd be upset. I was about go out for a week at the Great Banks, but I went to Suzie's condo and found him lying around, as usual. I told him to stay away from Rosie and that if he spoke to her, I'd have him arrested."

"And did he agree?"

"No, the bastard laughed in my face and told me it was too late."

"I've spoken to him, and we'll watch him closely. Did you or your wife run into him again?"

"Honestly, I haven't a clue, 'cause my memory after that is still blank."

The back door opened and Rosemary called, "Home, Dad!"

"We'll get out of your hair, then," Demaris said, rising. "And please call if we can assist tomorrow or if your memory returns and you have any other thoughts about the two deaths."

"Will do. She's a good girl, my Rosie," he whispered.

"Yes, she is. Take care, sir."

CHAPTER 36

Margery Franklin's service was held in the Catholic church in Mattapoisett and the reception after at the Center Street Gallery. She was to be cremated, but they were still holding her body in the small clinic morgue in case Megan Krieger needed to run further tests.

As usual, Demaris and Greta stood just outside the church door, Pete and Stevens inside. Peter and Carrie Thurbert arrived with Pru Marsden and her husband, Philip Randolph. Philip looked uncomfortable as he passed them.

"What's eating him?" Greta whispered. "Looks like he ate a lemon."

"I suspect Mr. Randolph prefers exotic locales to village life. Now he's being dragged to another funeral of someone he most likely never met."

"Too bad he's such a sourpuss. I like her."

Surprised, Demaris turned to his second-in-command.

"What, we can't make an innocent observation now and then?"

Her boss chuckled. "Observe away."

Garrett Rollins, Joan Nettleman, and Susan and Kevin LeBlanc, strolled past them. Jane Fellows and Bess followed their colleagues in. Becca Rollins came with her mother, Clarice, both dressed in flowing black. Lee Myers and Claire Rubin came together, no boyfriend or husband in sight. Palla Forest, unaccompanied, swished by them in a flowing black dress and shawl. Dennis Harrison entered alone—no surprise—and Vicky Brown was on the arm of an unfamiliar young man whom Demaris assumed was the estranged boyfriend, Derek Harper. Behind them came Suzanna and Barry Costa. He smirked as he passed by, daring them to detain him.

"What's his deal, sir?"

"Two-bit punk, thinks he's invincible," Pete said, coming up behind them. "A first-class jerk. Thinks he's a cock in the hen house, but I don't see any hens falling at his feet."

"Back inside, Pete. No more gossiping."

The traditional Catholic mass ended, and mourners filed out for the short two-block walk to the gallery. Bob and Rosemary had driven and were already inside waiting to have brief calling hours when Demaris and the others arrived. The book club ladies were bustling around, especially Betty Sue and Claire. "Where is the bartender?" Betty Sue asked, hands on hips, clearly irritated.

"He'll be here," Claire said. "I saw him leaving the church."

"Probably out back, having a cigarette," Betty Sue muttered. "Suzie's a sweetie, but I don't care for him."

"Ah, look," Claire said, pointing to the back door. "Here they are!"

Bob Franklin turned to see to whom Claire was pointing, his face instantly registering fury at the sight of Barry Costa. He left his daughter's side and crossed the room. "How dare you show your face here?"

"I'm workin'. Haven't you heard? Who do you think's tending bar?"

"Not you. Now get the hell out of here before I call the cops."

Claire Rubin stepped between the two men. "Perhaps it would be best if you leave, Barry."

"Look, I was hired for this gig and I expect to get paid."

As Demaris reached the group, he spied Pete already at Costa's side. "You heard Mr. Franklin," Demaris said. "Your presence is unwanted for very good reasons, and you will leave now without making a scene. My detective will escort you out the back door."

Pete laid hold of the man's arm, and Costa attempted to pull away. "Get your hands off me."

Pete ignored him and started for the door. Stevens grabbed the other arm and they dragged him out.

Suzanna came forward looking as if she might burst into tears. "He doesn't have a car. He came with me."

"Pete," he called. "You and Stevens drive him back to the condo and come back immediately."

"Will do, boss," Dugan said. "Come on, tough guy."

Demaris turned to Suzanna. "You okay?"

"Yes, thanks," she said, wiping her eyes with her serving apron.

"Sure you're okay?" Betty Sue asked, patting her shoulder. "We can handle things if need be."

"No, I'm fine, thanks. Won't be much fun going home tonight, but for all I know, Barry may take off and I won't see him again for another few years."

"I'll tend bar," Vicky Brown said, arm circling her friend's shoulders. "Was one of my many side jobs in college, so I shouldn't kill anyone."

"Thank you, dear," Claire said, eyes full of concern as she gazed from one woman to the other. "Are you sure?"

"Yes. It'll give me something to do. If I get stuck, I'm sure the person ordering the drink can give me instructions."

"Well, that crisis is over. You okay, Bob?"

"Thanks, Claire. I'll head over to help Rosie with the line. Lieutenant, can I speak with you afterward? I've just remembered something about last week that may or may not be important."

"Of course. When you're free, come find me. I'll be here. Detective Burke, too."

The room had filled, and he spied Bess with the group of school people and waved. She returned the wave, eyes questioning. The group had clearly observed the kerfuffle with Costa as they waited in line to express their condolences to the Franklins.

"Hello, Roger." Clarice Wills moved to his side. "Everything okay?"

"Right as things can be at a funeral."

She nodded as her eyes watched Becca, who stood with a group of her friends near the front door. "I'm still not sure why she insisted on coming, but here we are."

"I'm sorry. I haven't had time to talk with her. I will later today, if possible."

"She seems a bit calmer. Maybe I was imagining things."

"Probably not. How well did you know Marge Franklin?"

"Well enough. She was a voracious reader of mysteries. Something we shared. Before she married Bob, when she lived here in the village, she would stop in for a cup of tea on her way home from the gallery most afternoons."

"I'm surprised you aren't a member of the book club. All they read are mysteries, or so I hear."

"Same reason your wife isn't, I'd guess. Time and perhaps not the right disposition? Bess and I have actually talked about it. Knowing we love the genre, Claire and Marge have both invited us many times, but we always find an excuse. Maybe we're snobs?"

"I doubt that very much." He smiled at her as he spied Palla Forest approaching.

"Clarice, Lieutenant, hope this is the last of these for a while."

"Where's Wixie today?" he asked.

"My neighbor's watching her. I'm surprised Becca is here."

"She knew Marge and wanted to come," Clarice replied, her voice considerably icier than it had been several minutes earlier.

"Of course. Excuse me, will you?" Palla Forest hurried off to greet two strangers standing at the bar.

"Life with Garrett Rollins is never dull," Clarice whispered. "Better go check on Bec."

Rollins himself approached along with Greta. "Any progress?" he asked.

"Not so far. How's your daughter doing?"

"Bec? Okay. Still shaken up. Haven't seen Wixie today. Palla's holding her hostage."

"Do you think either girl saw more in the woods than she's been able to tell us?"

"Wixie, I doubt it, but Becca, maybe. She's been secretive and more sullen than usual since it happened, but some of that could be guilt over not watching Wixie more carefully. Palla's crap doesn't help."

"Was she privy to any of Ms. Forest's tirades?"

"No, but Wixie said something last week. Got Bec in a real funk."

"Is Becca staying with you tonight?"

"Who knows. She blows hot and cold. One minute she's glued to me, the next, her mother. Like Wixie, she's not overly fond of my girlfriend, Lily, but since that's a dead issue at the moment, no friction there."

"Oh?"

"She's moved out."

A group of school people, including Bess, approached them, some headed for the bar. Jane Fellows came forward first. "Am I allowed to hug the new husband?"

He laughed and embraced Bess's dear friend and colleague. "You're looking well, as always." And she was, in a long flowing dress, the fabric swirling blues and greens. Full-figured with bright green eyes, Jane was what one might call earthy.

"Not as well as you. I want to have you guys to dinner soon. You can come, too, Garrett, and bring Lily."

"Thanks, but Lily and I are taking a breather."

Jane gave Bess a look as the Thurberts came up to say hello, Joan Nettleman in their wake.

"Where's Pete?" Bess asked, stepping closer, hand on Demaris's arm.

"He and Stevens took Costa back to Old Harbor. Should be back soon."

"Hello, hello," Peter Thurbert said, extending his hand.

Demaris nodded, shaking his hand. "Mr. Thurbert, Ms. Thurbert, good to see you."

She barely acknowledged him and appeared bored, ready to bolt at the earliest opportunity. Carrie Thurbert's expression brightened when she spied Sue LeBlanc, her gym partner, and she waved. "Peter, I'll be over there. Come get me when you're ready to go." She practically sprinted across the room.

Her husband shrugged. "Exercise fanatics stick together. Quite a club. How's the investigation coming?"

"Slowly," Demaris replied, spying Becca Rollins out of the corner of his eye, headed their way. She looked frightened.

She reached around and pulled her father's sleeve. "Dad, I want to go, now, please."

"Bec, what's wrong?"

"Nothing, I just wanta go. Please!"

"What about your mom?"

"I want you to take me, now!"

Demaris stepped to her side. "Becca, has something frightened you?"

"No, I just want to go. Please, Dad!"

Rollins shrugged. "I guess we're going. Did you tell your mom?"

"Yes, now let's go!" She tugged at his sleeve, almost dragging him toward the door.

Demaris wanted to follow them, but without Pete and Brendan, he could not leave Greta alone. At that moment, a scream from the back of the gallery distracted his attention from the hasty departure of the Rollinses.

CHAPTER 37

Rosemary Franklin knelt beside her father, who had collapsed in a heap near the door to the office. "Dad, Dad! What's wrong, what's happened?"

"Call 911," Demaris said to Greta. "Tell them we need an ambulance here, now!"

Bob Franklin was limp and unresponsive, but still breathing. Demaris knelt and slapped his cheek. Franklin's eyes fluttered and he moaned. "Looks like he's been drugged or poisoned. Greta, phone that in so they're prepared. Then find out what he was drinking."

Chaos reigned as the EMTs arrived and loaded Franklin onto a stretcher. People all around them were crying and wringing their hands.

"Where're you taking him?" Demaris asked.

The beefy young man holding one end of the stretcher replied, "Northport General. They're prepared for drug overdose or poison."

"Good. We'll be there as soon as we can."

As the stretcher reached the front door, Pete and Stevens stepped in. Dugan raised his arms in a questioning gesture as he met his boss's eyes. Demaris crossed the room and barred the doorway. "You two stay here. No one leaves, understood? Greta and I will be in back. And Pete, call Megan and get her down here ASAP."

"Found this on the floor, sir." Greta held up a green plastic cup. Some of its contents had splattered across the tile.

"His?"

"Dunno. Vicky said he asked for iced tea. Looks like that's what's spilled here. Hard to say how much he drank."

"Did he eat anything?"

"Not that anyone noticed. Rosemary's been with him the whole time except when she excused herself and went to the bathroom. She left him sitting there," she said, indicating a table near the bar. One chair was on its side.

Demaris turned and waved to Vicky, who stood behind the bar. People still milled around, requesting drinks. She poured two glasses of lemonade and handed them to a woman, then came to stand next to Greta.

"Vicky, did you see anyone with Mr. Franklin while Rosemary was in the ladies' room?"

"There were people everywhere, stopping to speak to him, getting drinks. I was kind of swamped. It looked like he was, too. When I did glance over, he looked tired and seemed to be gulping down his tea. He looked really, really thirsty."

"Did he put anything in it?"

"Not that I saw. It was sweetened and had a lot of lemon. More than I'd have put," she whispered, eying the book club crew. "He could have put something else in it. As I said, I was pretty busy."

"Greta, get Pete and start talking to the people who were back here. See if anyone noticed who stopped to speak to Franklin. Get statements and their contact information, and then they can go. I want to talk to Harrison when you get to him. Brendan can man the front door."

Claire Rubin and Betty Sue approached, tears in their eyes. Lee Myers was right behind them. The other book club ladies were cleaning up, helping Suzanna to pack up the food. "We're starting to close things down, Lieutenant, unless you think we shouldn't?" Betty Sue said.

Claire nodded. "It seems a little pointless to continue this now that Rosemary and Bob have gone."

"I agree, but please pack up only what never came out of containers. Could you set all the platters, dishes, and trays that were passed on one of the tables? We'll box them up."

Betty Sue looked stricken. "You think he was poisoned with our food?"

"I haven't a clue, but until we know for certain why he passed out, we'll need to check everything. And that goes for the bar, too. Ask Vicky to stop serving and leave everything, and we'll collect it."

As the women went off to give instructions to the others, Greta turned to him. "You really think it was in the food?"

"No. I may be wrong, but I'd guess someone slipped something into his tea. Until we know for sure, all of it stays."

As Suzanna Costa set a half-full tray of sandwiches on the table, Demaris flagged her down. "Suzanna, have you been passing trays the whole time?"

"Since they took my brother away, yes."

"Did you see anyone near Bob Franklin when his daughter left him alone?"

"It was kind of a mob scene. There were a number of people around him, some I knew. I think a lot of them were Mattapoisett people. I was a little worried about him 'cause he looked exhausted. I offered to sit with him until Rosemary came back, but he said he was fine. Poor man. I hope he's okay. Maybe he checked out of the hospital too soon."

"Thanks, Suzanna. Please speak to Pete and help identify the Mattapoisett people you noticed."

"Oh, I just remembered something. The crowd from Old Harbor Friends was around him for a while. A bunch of them, including your wife. Then there was Derek. He was hangin' around.."

"Derek?"

"Derek Harper, Vicky's on-again, off-again boyfriend. I haven't the faintest idea why he came. Went right up to Mr. Franklin and hugged him."

"When was this?"

"In the receiving line. He worked for Mr. Franklin on one of the boats, but that was a while ago."

"Did Mr. Franklin seem happy to see him?"

"Not particularly."

"Did you see him later? When Mr. Franklin was sitting alone?"

"Well, he was hanging around the bar because of Vicky, but who knows whether he spoke to Mr. Franklin."

"Okay, thanks."

"Lieutenant, I know it's nothing compared to this, but did they say if they got Barry home safely?"

He gave her a kind smile. "I'm sure they did, but you can check with Pete." At that moment, his cell phone rang, and he excused himself and turned to answer. "What's that, Rollins? You're breaking up. I can't understand you. Becca saw what? Black what?" The line went dead.

When he turned back, Suzanna was still standing beside him, awaiting further instructions. "Oh, Suzanna, sorry about that. We're all set. If you want catch Pete before you start cleaning up, he's over there."

As he turned away, Dennis Harrison approached with Greta at his side. "Mr. Harrison, thanks for coming over."

"Like I had a choice."

"I wondered if you had any conversation with Bob Franklin before he passed out."

"What're you, nuts? Bob hates me. I only came for Marge, because she was an old friend."

"And lover, I believe?"

"What's your point?"

"My point is that people who become involved with you end up either dead or nearly so."

"Are you suggesting I had anything to do with what happened here?"

"I don't know. Did you?"

"I most certainly did not. I barely know this crowd, except for the Old Harbor people and a couple of guys from the golf club."

"I wonder why you came at all, then."

"As I said, I came to honor Marge."

"Maybe at the funeral mass, but here?"

"Look, I didn't go anywhere near Bob Franklin. Your detectives already asked what I saw. May I please get out of here?"

"Yes, you're free to go."

CHAPTER 38

As the last of the guests were ushered out, Claire and her crew behind them, Megan and Bethany arrived. Demaris breathed a sigh of relief at the sight of his forensic people. They could take over here. The rest of them were needed elsewhere.

"Meg, thanks for coming so quickly. Pete'll fill you in. I have to go outside and try to make a call."

He stepped out the rear door and punched "call back," hoping to reach Garrett Rollins, but the phone went directly to voice mail. He left a message asking him to call, then hung up and stepped back inside. Meg and Bethany were already loading boxes of food, Franklin's iced tea glass, and the rag Greta had used to mop up the spilled tea.

"I've got two guys coming from Crime Scene," Megan said as she began loading open bottles and sealing open pitchers from the bar with plastic wrap and tape. "What're you thinking?"

"That he was drugged. Whether the intent was to kill him or just knock him out, I'm not sure. Greta and I are headed to the hospital now. We should know more when we get there."

"No word, then?"

"No, and I called Chief Smith. He sent a man over there. He was to call if there was any news."

"What about me?" Pete asked. "Greta can stay here and mop up with Stevens."

Taking a deep breath, Demaris turned to his second-in-command. "Meg and Bethany are the only ones staying here. I need you and Stevens to head to Old Harbor and pick up Garrett and Becca Rollins right away."

"Why?"

"Because I said so. If my hunch is correct, they're both in grave danger. Now get Stevens and go. Try the dorm first. Then scour the campus and town until you find them, *comprende?*"

Pete opened his mouth to protest, but then said, "Okay, will do," and turned away to grab Stevens, who was helping Bethany load boxes into the van.

*****

When they reached the hospital, they were directed to the second floor and asked to wait. After fifteen minutes, a blond thirty something doctor in lime-green scrubs appeared with Chief Smith at his side. "Hey, Roger," the chief said. "Don't worry. My officer's at Franklin's door."

"Mr. Franklin was very lucky," the young doctor said. "He had enough diazepam in him to fell an elephant. We were able to pump his stomach. Another half hour and we'd have lost him."

"Is he going to be okay?"

"I think so, but he'll be asleep for twelve hours at least."

"Any idea how the diazepam was administered?"

"Looks like someone spiked his iced tea. Wasn't much else in his stomach except cracker crumbs. Funny he didn't notice the taste. That much and it would have made the tea really bitter."

"So there's no way to bring him out sooner, then?"

"Not really. And even if we slapped him around, he would be so groggy you wouldn't get a sensible word out of him."

Demaris turned to his friend. "Can your man stay with him?"

"As long as he's here."

"His daughter's with him, too," said the doctor.

"Thanks. We'll take off, then. Paul, if you can ask your man to call me when Franklin's awake and coherent, I'd be grateful."

"You got it. Good luck."

*****

"What're you thinking, boss?" Greta asked as they crossed the hospital parking lot.

"That Garrett and Becca Rollins are in terrible danger, and I hope Pete and Brendan have found them."

He called Pete, and his assistant picked up on the first ring. "Have you found them?"

"I spoke to Rollins, and he agreed to get Becca and meet us at the guest house."

"Didn't I ask you to pick them up?"

"He insisted that we had to do it this way, Rodge. Believe me, we tried."

"And?"

"Looks like they made it to the guest house. There was some kind of struggle, and one or both of them was dragged out."

"Jesus Christ, check with Tilly and Rach. See if they saw anything."

"Just came through there, and no one at the Tavern noticed anything. Place half empty except that cocky bastard, Costa, at the bar."

"I'll call Chief Wilbur and have his men assist you. Turn that goddamn village upside down and inside out till you locate them. Do you hear me, Pete? And you and Brendan stay together."

"Will do."

After phoning Wilbur, who agreed to send his men out, Demaris called Bess. She answered immediately. "Hi. I barely saw you at the gallery. Is Bob okay?"

"Looks like he'll pull through. Bess, where are you?"

"Just heading down to my car. A group of us came back to the village together, and we sat around the Commons talking for a bit. Garrett was with us. He seemed very agitated. We were trying to help."

"Who was with you?"

"Jane, Joan, Peter, and Kevin LeBlanc."

"What was Rollins agitated about?"

"He wouldn't say. Just that it had something to do with Becca. He was supposed to meet her, but she wasn't answering her cell phone. Kept saying she'd seen something, but he didn't explain."

"Did he finally reach her?"

"No, all of a sudden he said he had to go and ran off."

"But Rollins and Becca left the gallery together. How did they get separated?"

"Becca asked to be dropped off at her mom's. She'd forgotten her cell and she wanted to show him something. They were planning to meet up, but she never called."

"Jesus Christ, where are the rest of them?"

"Peter, Joan, and Kevin went out to Ahab's for dinner."

"What about Jane?"

"Walking right beside me. Why?"

"I want you both to get in the car and drive to the B and B. Stay with Lois and Cathy until I call. Do you understand?"

"Why?"

"Bess, just do it!"

"But—"

"Call me when you're safe at the B and B."

"Roger, please tell me what's wrong."

"I don't know, but I want to be sure you're safe. I'll explain later. I've got to go."

He rang off and phoned Lois, whom he knew possessed a gun and understood how to use it. She promised to phone the second Bess and Jane arrived.

"Fast as you can, Greta," Demaris said.

"Where to?"

"Village Books."

Greta didn't ask, but she pushed the speed limit as they headed back to town.

CHAPTER 39

As they reached the village, Demaris's phone rang. It was Lois letting him know that Bess and Jane had arrived safely.

"Good. Thanks, Lo."

"Cathy just saw something odd, Roger."

"Oh?"

"Suzanna Costa practically ran her over on Main Street. Cathy said it looked like Garrett Rollins was with her. Odd couple, don't you think? Cathy said the man looked like a ghost."

"Jesus Christ, let me speak to Cathy."

Lois's partner came on immediately. "Hey, Roger."

"Which direction was Costa headed?"

"Out of town. Last I saw, she had turned onto the Coast Road."

"Thanks, Cath. All of you stay put!" He turned to Greta. "Forget the book shop. Head for the Coast Road and hope we aren't too late."

He dialed Pete to find out what kind of car Suzanna Costa drove.

"Honda CR-V, black," Dugan said. "Is she mixed up in this?"

"I'm afraid so. Pete, stop at Village Books. Clarice is probably still there. If she's not at the shop, she lives on Long Lane, red farmhouse next to the Grange. Find her and ask if she's heard from Becca. Tell her to call me."

"Yes, sir."

Demaris hung up. "We're looking for a black Honda SUV."

"Yes, sir." Greta took the turn and headed north on the Coast Road.

Demaris called the Tavern, and Tilly told him Barry Costa was still at the bar, drinking shots of tequila with beer chasers. "Call the police station and have someone pick him up. Tell them I asked them to hold him. If they refuse, call me."

"He's already drunk himself under the table, Roger."

"Still, I want him where I can find him. Thanks, Till."

As they raced along in the growing twilight, they passed few cars and no black Hondas. "Where the hell are they?" he asked as they neared the turn for Osprey Point.

"Should we check up there, sir?"

"Yeah, go ahead. We're groping in the dark anyway."

They reached the Point and spied two bikes but no cars. "Dammit," he said as Greta backed up and his cell phone rang.

"Hey, boss," Pete said. "We're with Clarice Wills. She hasn't heard from Becca or Garrett and she's out of her mind. Stevens had an idea, though. He called Rollins' cell and was able to run a trace. Not exact, but it looks like Rollins, at least, is somewhere near Devil's Cove."

"Thanks, Pete, on our way. We could use some company."

"Be there in ten." Dugan clicked off.

"Devil's Cove, Greta. I don't know why I didn't think of it. Much more secluded. She'd have lots of cover. Make a U-turn up here. The turnoff is about eight miles back the way we came."

As Greta sped in a semicircle, he gazed ahead. "If we didn't pass them comin' down, they've had a really good head start, dammit."

Five minutes later, they turned onto the gravel road leading to a public park and secluded cove known for its beautiful surrounding woods and great fishing. When they rounded the last bend in the road, they spied the SUV parked at an odd angle on the soft embankment leading down to the cove. As Greta stopped and they jumped out, they heard a scream coming from the woods.

"Let go of me, you bitch!" Becca Rollins screamed. "What have you done to my dad?"

As Demaris and Greta entered the woods, Pete's jeep appeared. He and Stevens hopped out, a local police cruiser right behind them.

CHAPTER 40

About a hundred yards into the woods, they came upon a strange scene. Suzanna had Becca's legs, still tied together, and was dragging her toward a trench. Garrett Rollins lay beside it, either drugged or dead. As yet, neither had been strangled.

"It's over, Suzanna. Let her go!" Demaris called.

Costa looked up, eyes wild with fury and hatred. "Go to hell!"

She reached back, pulling a pistol from the waist of her jeans. As she aimed, Pete fired. She dropped Becca's legs and fell forward, her body covering the girl.

Becca screamed, "Get off me, you bitch!" and threw Costa's limp body aside, crawling toward her father, who lay still and lifeless beside the trench. "Daddy, Daddy, please, Daddy."

Rollins moaned and opened his eyes. Becca threw herself on him, sobbing, as Suzanna rose up on one elbow, pistol in her right hand. Before she could fire, Stevens tackled her and knocked the gun clear.

"Oh, no you don't!" he said, pinning her down.

Pete's bullet had hit her in the chest, and blood began to pool next to Rollins.

Greta stepped forward and untied Becca's ankles. "Ambulance is on its way, boss."

"Good. Let's get him up. Since he's coming to, we'll drive him. Let the ambulance take her. Brendan, you ride with them."

"Yes, sir."

"Greta, let's get Rollins to the car. You and Becca can take him to the hospital. Pete and I will be along soon. Good work, everyone."

Unconscious now, Suzanna Costa was loaded into the ambulance. Stevens hopped up beside her just as Greta drove off with father and daughter.

"Pete," Demaris asked, "Do you have Clarice Wills's number?"

Dugan nodded.

"Call her. Tell her they're safe and headed for Northport General."

Pete nodded again and made the call, turning back to find his boss staring at the open trench.

"Good shot," Demaris said softly. "And Brendan deserves a commendation. If not for his quick thinking, we never would have found them."

"He's definitely a keeper, boss."

"You have Costa's gun?"

"Yup."

"Then let's go."

"Home?"

"No, Northport General. I just got a text. Bob Franklin's awake and lucid."

CHAPTER 41

En route to Northport, Demaris phoned Chief Wilbur and was assured that Barry Costa was in custody and would remain so overnight. He then called Bess and told her it was safe for her and Jane to go home.

It was dark when they arrived at the hospital and headed to Franklin's room. When they reached it, they found him dozing, Rosemary at his side. Chief Smith's officer was standing guard. Demaris nodded to him. "Hope we'll be able to send you home soon."

Rosemary hopped up and came to hug first Dugan, then Demaris. "Thank you. He would have died if you hadn't been there."

Demaris returned her embrace as he patted her back. "We've apprehended the person we think killed your stepmother."

"Who?"

"Suzanna Costa."

"Suzie? Why would she want to harm Marge? And Gretchen was like a mom to her."

"That's why we're here, hoping your dad remembered something that might help us, 'cause she's not talking."

"I did remember something," he said, raising the bed so he could sit up.

"How're you feeling?" Demaris asked.

"Like I've been hit by a bus, again. Memory's back, though, or at least some of it."

Demaris sat in one of the two chairs beside the bed. "Why don't you tell us?"

"Gretchen came to dinner last week. She and Marge were going to have lunch, but I suggested she come for dinner, and I grilled lobsters. Gretchen and I hardly knew each other, but I had something I wanted to tell her. Something I've been carrying a long time. Rosie, would you be an angel and go get your dad something good from the cafeteria? Better than the crap I'll get for lunch."

No fool, Rosemary sat in the other chair. "I can handle it, Dad. Please let me stay."

Her father regarded her with sad eyes, then said, "I know you can, baby, but I hate to have you relive the crap Barry Costa put you through."

"I'm fine," she said, sitting up straighter.

He shrugged. "Okay, sweetie. After what you've been through the past week, I guess this is pretty tame. Anyway, this all happened years ago, when Barry Costa was taking advantage of my young, impressionable fourteen-year-old.

"As I told you earlier, I hated Costa and didn't trust him, so I hired a private investigator to follow him, to look into everything about the scumbag. The guy I hired was terrific. He looked into all Costa's shady business dealings, his relationship with his sister, and basically trailed him for almost two months. It was during the time when Gretchen was married to Greg Parker. Parker was kind of a scumbag himself, in my opinion, but I didn't know how bad he was until I got the guy's report.

"Basically, Costa and his sister are grifters, and have worked scams on a number of people over the years. He drags her in on his schemes during the summer months when school's out. Always someplace far from here. They each have several aliases, him more than her. They started real young, since their mother was a useless drug addict in and out of jail and rehab. They stayed alone at home for long stretches while Mommy Dearest led her crappy, good-for-nothing life.

"Anyway, the brother needed money that summer to travel west for some big scam, so he persuaded Suzie to seduce Greg Parker. Wasn't difficult. She was living on and off with the Parkers then 'cause she and Vicky had become friends. Apparently, a few days of traipsing around in her underwear and Suzie had Greg in the sack. Went on for a week or two. Then Barry stepped in. Told Parker he would expose him and ruin him if he didn't pay up, big.

"Greg Parker had money, lots of it, but instead of paying the blackmail from his own filthy pockets, he started stealing Gretchen's jewelry. He'd give it to Costa. They'd have copies made. Then Costa fenced the originals. This went on until he had enough to get outta town. Poor Vicky knew nothing about it, and neither did Gretchen until last week when I told her. She said she planned to confront Suzanna and ask for restitution."

Demaris shook his head. "And if she confronted Suzanna, she most likely intended to tell Vicky."

"Yes, poor Gretchen. I never cared for her, mostly because of her connection to Dennis Harrison. He treated my Margie like shit. I would wager he gave the same, if not worse, to all his wives."

"Yes, we've heard that about Mr. Harrison," Demaris said.

"So Suzanna hasn't said a thing?"

"Not yet."

"Do you have enough to charge her?"

"I hope so. Police are searching the condo and her car right now. Either way, she'll serve considerable time for the kidnapping and attempted murder of Rollins and Becca."

"Glad you found them in time. He's kind of a snob, but Becca's a sweetheart."

"Yes, she is. Who was the PI you employed to follow Costa?"

"Will Kaplan, in Taunton. Real nice guy. We kept in touch. He passed away last year. Lung cancer. I think his son took over the business."

"Well, we'll let you rest. Thanks."

"Good luck knockin' the truth out of them."

*****

They headed to the ER, where Garrett Rollins was just being released. Clarice and Becca sat beside him on the hospital bed. When Becca spied Demaris, her face brightened, and she jumped up to hug him.

"Hey, you're safe now, sweetheart. How're you doing?"

"They gave me an ice pack and some aspirin. Feels better."

"She's my brave girl," Rollins said.

Tears in her eyes, Clarice looked up at Demaris.

"How's Mom holding up?" he asked.

Clarice looked stricken. "Oh, Roger, when I think what might have happened if you hadn't found them."

Demaris sat beside her, his arm circling her shoulders. She leaned against him and broke into sobs.

"Hey, hey, everyone's safe. And you can thank Officer Stevens when you see him. It was his quick thinking that helped us find them.

"You feel up to telling us what happened?" he asked, looking from father to daughter.

They both nodded, and Rollins began. "As you know, Becca was freaked out after the funeral. It was the shoes, Spiderman's shoes. Turns out, she snapped a blurry photo of Spiderman's feet in the woods that day, but didn't want to tell anyone. Then, she spied someone at the gallery wearing those same kind of sneakers. That weird brand with the two red stripes on the outside and red stripes in the soles."

"Wolf Runners," Pete said.

"That's it. Bec recognized them as the same kind worn by the person the girls saw in the woods. She found me and wanted to leave, get her cell phone at her Mom's and show me. Was stupid. We should have spoken to you then rather than coming back to the village. Suzanna must have overheard us talking to you. Anyway, on the way back, Bec told me about the sneakers, but refused to tell me who was wearing them. Insisted she wanted to tell you herself. So that's when I called you.

"Then your detectives called and asked us to meet them at the guest house. I figured there was no rush and left Becca at her mom's to get the phone. We arranged to meet in twenty minutes. I drove home, let the dog out. It's Lily's. I agreed to keep it while she's away. Anyway, I put him back in the apartment and jogged over to the guest house. When I arrived, Suzanna was just getting into her car. She said she was coming to talk with you, but no one was around. I asked if she'd seen Bec and she said no, but offered to drive me to Clary's.

"She had a cooler on the floor. I was thirsty from the jog, and she said I could help myself. I grabbed a bottle of iced tea and gulped it down. Just as I started to conk out, I glanced in the backseat and saw the sneakers. I tried to grab the wheel and we fought. I think we almost ran someone over."

"Cathy Nolan."

"Is she okay?"

"Yes. She told us that you were with Suzanna."

"I blacked out then."

Demaris turned to Becca. "Can you tell us what happened to you?"

"I knocked on the door of the guest house and no one answered, so I opened it. She must have been behind the door. I don't remember anything else until she was dragging me in the woods. Then I saw Dad. I thought he was dead."

"Okay, that's enough for now. I don't suppose Suzanna said anything to either of you?"

"Nothing except shut up and stuff like that," she said.

"We didn't recover a cell phone at the scene. Do you have it?"

"No."

"I suspect it's been tossed in the river, but we'll check into it." He smiled at Becca and her parents. "We'll let you get going. I'm sure you'll all be glad to get home. Do you need a ride?"

"I've got this one," Clarice Wills said. "Come on, gang."

They watched the three head out. Then Demaris turned to Pete.

"Okay, partner, ready to see how Ms. Costa's doing?"

CHAPTER 42

The surgeon who had removed Pete's bullet from Suzanna Costa's side was just closing the door to her room when they arrived. Stevens stepped from his post at the door. "Dr. Carroll, this is my boss, Lieutenant Demaris, from R.H.D."

The barrel-chested, balding, middle-aged Carroll nodded. "You'll want to talk to her, I imagine."

"How is she?" Demaris asked.

"Very cranky, mouth of a longshoreman, but she'll make it. Lost a lot of blood, but the bullet passed through and lodged against a rib bone without damaging any critical organs. We were able to remove it. She's been given a sedative, so she'll be out pretty soon. Morning might be preferable if you want her to make any sense."

"Thanks, doc. We'll be brief."

The doctor disappeared and Demaris stared at the closed door. After several minutes, he said, "You know what? I think the doctor's right. Let's wait till morning. Brendan, are you okay here?"

Stevens nodded. "Yes, sir."

"Would you like Pete, Greta, or one of the Old Harbor guys to relieve you in a few hours?"

"If it's all the same to you, sir, I'd like to see this through until you come back in the morning. Nurses have been feeding me and bringing coffee, so I'm all set."

"Good man. Brendan, you did exceptional work today."

"Thank you, sir."

"If you start to flag, all three of us will have our cell phones on throughout the night."

"Yes, sir."

"I can stay with him, boss," Pete said.

Demaris hesitated, not wanting to undermine Stevens, but safety won out. "Good idea. Brendan, this is not about your ability. After last year, I've made it a priority not to leave my people alone."

"Yes, sir," Stevens replied, not looking the least bit offended to be spending the night working alongside his idol.

"Brendan, did they find a cell phone in Suzanna's things?"

"No, sir. Her purse got tossed into the ambulance and it's bagged now, but there wasn't much in it."

"Not in the car, either. If Crime Scene doesn't find it, I expect she tossed both Becca's phone and her own."

"Okay, then, you two. Take care and call if you need us."

They left Pete and Stevens sitting side by side outside Suzanna Costa's room.

"Two peas in a pod," Greta whispered as she followed her boss into the elevator.

CHAPTER 43

As the sun rose early Friday morning, they lay in each other's arms, neither wanting to make the first move to start the day. Finally, Bess rose on one elbow. "Did Mary say what time she'd be in?"

"They land around three-thirty. I offered to pick them up, but her friend Nancy's getting them. They'll come straight here, so I'd guess around four-thirty?"

"I can definitely be home by then, but I don't think Mary will be pleased if you're not here to greet them."

"Not to worry. I'll be home in plenty of time. I've got the Costa interviews, but we're wrapping up."

"Has anyone talked to poor Vicky? She must be devastated to think her dear friend could do such a thing."

"Pete texted and said that Hillary went over last night. I know they offered to stay with her, but she said she was fine. Hillary helped her pack up all Suzanna's things and put them in Pete's car. Hill will drop them off this morning, and we'll sift through, but we probably won't find much. She's a pro."

"I just can't believe it," Bess said. "All those years she's lived in the village and she's been off every summer doing those horrible things with Barry."

"Card-carrying grifters are an amazing bunch. They are able to live day to day fooling the pants off people, even those close to them."

"Has the school been notified that Suzanna is in custody?"

"Yup, Greta got the principal last night. He was already fixing to write her up for missing so much school. She called in sick last Wednesday, when she was killing and trying to dispose of Ms. Parker. Then she left at noon last Thursday for her trip to Mattapoisett to kill Marge."

"And poor Pete and Brendan spent all night at the hospital?"

"I didn't want to leave Brendan alone. They're young, and they probably took shifts dozing and keeping watch."

"You have a wonderful team."

"Yes, I do."

"It's a terrible burden, trying to keep them safe, isn't it?"

"Yes." He kissed her nose and slid out of bed. "Sorry, my dearest, but duty calls."

"Do you want my car since yours is who knows where?"

"Parked at the guest house. No, Greta's picking me up. Should be here soon."

"What about breakfast?"

"No time, my love. Tilly will feed us when we return from Northport. Greta's picking up coffee."

He showered and dressed quickly. Still in her robe, Bess came to say goodbye. At the door, he drew her close, soaking in her warmth as they kissed. "After this weekend, it's going to be honeymoon number two, I promise. Any chance you could take a day or two off?"

"Not at this time of year, but I'll try to arrange things so I can come home early."

"And I will have dinner waiting. Have a good day, sweetheart."

"You, too."

*****

As Demaris and Greta drove into Northport, he asked, "Have you got all your notes and Brendan's?"

She nodded.

"What about Bob Franklin's files?"

"Got it all, boss. We're ready. Just phoned Pete, and he says Costa's up and swearing at everyone who comes near her. Tried to get out of bed and find her clothes, which the hospital threw away after cutting them off her."

"Good work. What about the brother?"

"Chief Wilbur has him locked up and will keep him there until we get back." She turned in and parked at Northport General.

"Okay," he said. "Here goes nothing."

*****

When Demaris and Greta stepped out of the elevator, both Pete and Stevens were sitting in the hall outside Suzanna Costa's room. Both had large coffees and what appeared to be remnants of sugar doughnuts in their hands. "Hey, boss," Pete said, grinning like the Cheshire cat. Pete loved overnight jobs, and it was clear that he and Stevens had been happy as clams guarding the prisoner.

"How're things?"

"We're in a bit of a mood in there, which is why Brendan and I are out here. We were afraid she might start throwing things."

Demaris reached out and Greta handed him her files. "Okay, then, let's see if we can make Ms. Costa more pissy than she already is. Greta's with me. Brendan, I want you to head back with Pete. Order breakfast if you're still hungry. I'll get something when I get back. Chief Smith's guy should be here any minute to stand guard."

Dugan stood up, powdered sugar spilling down his front. "But boss, I should be in there."

"These are Greta's notes," Demaris said, holding up the files. "She knows them, and I need her in there. I want you and Brendan to go back to the guest house and start sifting through Suzanna Costa's belongings. Hillary has already dropped them off. We may need them in this interview, so hurry, please. Text Greta anything you find, understood?"

"But, boss, we've been here all night and—"

"And you can take a nap later. Now, go."

Stevens and Burke stood silent, observing the familiar tug of war between their boss and his hot-headed second-in-command. No one could speak to the boss like Pete did and live to see another day. The word *brat* came to mind.

"Greta, let's go," Demaris said, pushing open the door.

She shrugged at Pete, whom she knew would not speak to her for the rest of the day.

<h1 style="text-align:center">CHAPTER 44</h1>

Costa was sitting up, holding a small hand mirror as she brushed her hair. "Get the hell out. I know my rights and I don't have to talk to you."

"Have you phoned your attorney, then?"

"What the fuck for?"

"Well, we're happy to wait for him or her, but otherwise, Ms. Costa, yes, you do need to speak with us. Or at least listen to what's in store for you."

"Get on with it then, and be quick about it. I want to get out of here and get back to work. I don't know what they must be thinking. I haven't been able to call since I can't find my cell, and they refuse to give me a phone in this dump."

Demaris stared at her, not quite believing what they were hearing. Was the woman delusional? Did she forget that they found her dragging Becca Rollins and her father to the grave she had dug? "It was my order that the phone be removed."

"Figures."

"And I wouldn't concern yourself with your job. You've been fired, and a long-term sub is already in place."

"What the hell are you talking about?"

"Ms. Costa, why do you think you're in the hospital?"

"Because that idiot Dugan shot me. Wait'll I see him around the condos."

"Are you seriously going to sit there and tell us you don't know why you were shot?"

"Fuck off."

"So far, you are being held for the kidnapping and attempted murder of Becca and Garrett Rollins. Those charges alone will send you to jail for a very long time."

"Says you. I know how the system works."

"As I was saying, you will be charged for the aforementioned crimes, and I feel confident that you will also be charged with the murders of Gretchen Parker and Margery Franklin."

"Dream on." Despite her attempts to smooth her hair, the woman looked like a stuffed bird whose feathers had been caught in a blender.

"My detectives are going through your car and all your possessions and your brother's as we speak. We will find evidence, in addition to the eye witness who saw and recognized you."

"How dare you touch my things. Vicky wouldn't allow it!"

"Ms. Brown helped pack it all up. Couldn't get your things out of the condo fast enough."

"She would never do that, unless you've told her a bunch of lies."

"Then, there's the forensic evidence, I'm certain we'll find at the condo. We have a team going over it as we speak. But, let's leave that for a moment." He opened the files in his lap, slowly flipping through them. "Let's talk about Mr. Kaplan's report for a moment."

"Who the hell is he?"

"Will Kaplan was the private investigator Bob Franklin hired to look into your brother's activities. He was quite thorough. So, who were you last summer, Angela Douglas? Or was it Lois Hadley? You've probably accumulated a whole slew of new names since Kaplan was following your brother."

"You have no idea what the hell you're talking about."

"We have someone appraising all Gretchen Parker's jewelry."

"What does that have to do with me or Barry?"

"You stole the originals and had copies made."

"Greg Parker stole his wife's jewelry, not me or Barry."

Demaris smiled slightly as he gazed into her cold green eyes. "How would you know about that if you weren't involved?"

"Vicky told me."

"She knew nothing about the thefts until we told her last night."

"Bullshit."

"That jewelry, which she had secured in her safe deposit box, represented her inheritance. Why would she lock it up if she knew it was worthless?"

"People do strange things."

"She also didn't know about your seduction of Greg Parker and the blackmail."

"Parker came after me. Practically raped me."

"Then you admit to the affair?"

"Big deal. Had a few very boring fucks with the old geezer, then told him to take a hike."

"Was this before or after your brother began blackmailing him?"

"Never happened."

"Was it before or after Barry visited Campbell Blake, the jewelry maker, and ordered copies of several rings, necklaces, and bracelets? Mr. Blake always photographs his work. He also keeps meticulous records, including video images of all his customers. Has years of film. It's quite impressive."

"Yeah, right."

"And then there are the two pawn shops to which Will Kaplan traced the stolen items. They, too, keep good records, and they identified your brother as the seller."

"Blah, blah, blah. None of this will hold up in court."

"But an eye witness who places you in the woods in your Spiderman getup standing over Gretchen Parker's body will be quite credible. Then there are your fingerprints on Dennis Harrison's golf bag."

"Not possible."

"Why? Did you wear gloves?"

"Go to hell."

"You were careful with the outside, but my forensic team lifted two clear prints from the inside of the bag."

"Bullshit."

Demaris's cell phone rang and he said, "Will you excuse me?" as he stepped out into the hall.

When he returned, he sat down and scribbled notes for a few minutes before looking up at Costa. "That was my detective. They found the garrote handles in your trunk. I'm quite certain the blood found on them will belong to Gretchen Parker and Margery Franklin. Give it up, Ms. Costa. It's over. The only thing left is for you to tell us whether your brother was involved. He's being detained at the moment, awaiting questioning."

"Barry knows nothing about any of this!"

"Any of what?"

"Gretchen, Marge, the Rollins kid."

"So you planned and carried out everything yourself?"

"Yes. I did it for him. Gretchen was going to tell Vicky about Greg and the jewelry. Then she'd probably blab it all over town. I couldn't let that happen. Barry has a fear of small spaces. He will die in prison. I know he will."

Demaris stood. "Detective Burke will stay with you while you write out and verbally describe your role in the murders of Gretchen Parker and Margery Franklin as well as the attempted murders of Lee Myers, Garrett Rollins, and Becca Rollins. After that, an officer will remain with you until you are well enough to be remanded to Delcar Prison to await trial. If your brother corroborates your story, there is a good chance that his sentence for the jewel theft and blackmail will be light."

"Didn't you hear me? My brother's severely claustrophobic. He cannot be placed in confined spaces."

"He should have thought of that long ago. Good day, Ms. Costa."

CHAPTER 45

"So, how go the first weeks of marriage?" Jane Fellows asked. "Not exactly the honeymoon you guys had planned. Now his kids are coming for the weekend?"

The two friends usually met for lunch every Friday in the Commons. Aside from their time at the past week's funerals, they had seen little of each other since Bess's marriage. On this warm day, they had taken their sandwiches out to sit on the grass of the campus green. A sheltered spot, surrounded on three sides by tall hedgerows, it was one of Bess's favorite places on campus.

"I suspect life with a police officer is seldom, if ever, predictable, but what about my life has ever been? Who could have predicted dear Harry's terrible death? And now Gretchen Parker's not a hundred feet away?"

"Technically, Parker wasn't killed there, but in the apartment, right?"

"Yes."

"Let's leave the grisly subject, shall we? Tell me about the kids."

"Owen and Terry? They're great. Terry hasn't quite warmed to me, but I hope with time we'll become friends. Owen is a sweetheart, and he worships his dad."

"I envy you, my friend. Don't s'pose a husband or kids are in my future. You think you and Roger'll have any of your own?"

"I'd guess not, at our ages."

"Still possible."

"Maybe."

"Have you talked about it?"

"Honestly, no. I don't think he wants more children."

"What about you?"

"I don't know. Mac never wanted children. Harry, maybe. But at our ages, we'd be in our sixties when a child went off to college."

"Then you'll be all the wiser in dealing with them."

Bess laughed. "Can we talk about something else? I made a decision this week."

"About?"

"About the Anne Greyson books. As you know, Roger and Mr. Winthrop have been after me to consider continuing the books. Harry's publisher, too."

"And?"

"I thought I might start by taking a writing course at UMass Dartmouth. Then there's a writers' retreat next spring on Gooseberry Island. I thought I'd go and see if I can make a start. In the meantime, I'm going to reread all the books. If I still feel confident after that, I'll forge ahead. I actually have an idea for a new adventure for Helen." She referred to the series' main character and amateur sleuth, Helen Brown.

"Great. Do tell!"

"Not yet. I'd like to let it percolate a little first before I run it by anyone."

"Does Roger know?"

"No. He's been so busy, I haven't wanted to bother him. Besides, I just made the decision yesterday. It'll give me something to do when he's off on a case. As you know, he can often be at it for days or weeks."

"I love it! Maybe you can get that hunky Tim Hargreaves down to brainstorm with you. I wouldn't mind seeing him again." A dear friend and traveling companion of Bess' former fiancé, Harry Winthrop, Hargreaves had helped his friend develop the mystery series. Following Winthrop's murder, Hargreaves had spent several weeks in the village, charming more than one female.

Bess studied her beautiful, accomplished friend, who had wasted nearly a decade in a relationship with the former married headmaster, Peter Thurbert. "That's not a bad idea, although Tim is a bit fickle, don't you think?"

"I'll take anyone at this point."

"What's happened with the online stuff?"

"Nothing, zip, zero."

"Well, don't give up, Jane."

"I won't. Uh-oh, here comes Garrett. Probably wants to go on and on about his near-death experience."

"Hey, ladies, can I join you?"

"Of course," Bess said. "How are you feeling?"

"Much better now that I know Becca is safe. When I think what could have happened. It's made me completely rethink my priorities."

"Oh? In what way?" Jane gave Bess a look over his shoulders.

"Well, for one, I'm going to break things off with Lily permanently. I mean, she's already moved out, but when she gets back from her trip, the dog goes and that's it. She's insanely too young for me. I realized driving back last night that

I gave up so much in divorcing Clarice. She probably won't have me back, but maybe we can be better friends."

"Clary is a wonderful person," Bess said. "I know Roger considers her a dear friend, and so do I."

"How's Becca doing?" Jane asked, mentally weighing the pros and cons of dating the peripatetic archivist, who changed jobs and women with every season. She ultimately concluded that Rollins was a poor dating prospect.

"Bec's a trooper. She fought like hell with that insane woman, mostly trying to save me."

Bess nodded. "She was very brave, and we're so glad you're both okay."

"Well, time to get back to class," Jane said, standing and brushing crumbs from her sea-green tunic.

"Oh, my goodness," Bess said. "Is that the time? My sophomores will have torn up the studio by now." She hopped up, and Rollins followed suit. "Sorry, we have to run, Garrett."

"We're not on a flexible schedule like our resident archivist," Jane quipped.

"Bye, ladies. See you around."

When Bess looked back and waved, Rollins was still standing in place, watching their retreat, looking lost and wistful.

CHAPTER 46

When Demaris and Greta got back to the guest house, Vicky Brown was sitting with Pete and Stevens. He greeted her warmly. "Vicky, how're you holding up?"

"Truthfully, not all that well, but Derek's been really supportive."

"Harper?"

"Yes. I know he has a bad reputation, and as you know, my mom hated him, but he's changed. He started going to AA two years ago, and he's been clean and sober ever since. Has a good job working for Steele Harrison. Loves the landscaping business. It was really kind of Steele to take him on, given my mom's history with his father. We're taking it slow, but it sure is nice to have a friend when you've just lost your dearest friend and your mother. How could I not have known about Suzie and Barry?"

"The Costas are as close to pros as I've seen in my years as a police officer. We don't deal with big-time cases involving grifters, but I've read enough about 'em. They've been leading double lives since their early teens. It's not unlike bigamists who have spouses in two places."

"She was so supportive after Mom and they were always so close."

"Yes," he said quietly.

"Well, I'll let you get on with your work. Are you packing up?"

"Yup. Most likely we'll be here through Monday."

"Thank you, all four of you." Tears in her eyes, Vicky Brown turned away.

"Take care," he said, as the others echoed his sentiments.

*****

"So, what've we got?"

"Costa admitted to the Parker blackmail and theft," Pete said. "But it doesn't appear that he knew anything about little sister's recent extracurricular activities. He was shocked. Even for a consummate actor, his surprise looked genuine."

"That's consistent with Suzanna's version, but then, she wants to protect him."

"We've got her, boss," Dugan said. "With the bloody garrote handles, Parker's blood in her trunk, and the fingerprints on the golf bag, we probably won't even need Becca Rollins's testimony."

"I hope not. Thoughts, Brendan?"

"No, sir. Pete pretty much covered it."

"Greta?"

"Think that's it, boss," she said, closing her laptop.

"Well, good work, everyone. Northport cops have taken over the guard detail from Chief Smith's men. They'll stay with Suzanna Costa until she's well enough to be transferred to Delcar. Barry will probably get off on the Parker charges, but there's an outstanding warrant for him in New Jersey, so he may do some time somewhere."

"Poor guy with his claustrophobia," Greta said without a hint of sarcasm. When she saw the others were staring, she said, "What? Claustrophobia is not a joke, you know."

"You?" Pete said.

"I control it. Let's leave it at that," she said.

"Okay," Demaris said. "Subject closed. Good work, everyone. Brendan, I am putting you up for a commendation. I have no doubt that the Garrett Rollins and his daughter would be dead were it not for your quick thinking and technological wizardry."

"Thank you, sir."

All three clapped as Stevens blushed crimson.

"Let's pack up for today," he said. "I've got my kids coming and I want to get home. Greta, we'll leave things till Monday. It's your choice if you want to go home or stay on for the weekend."

"If you don't mind, I think I'll stay. I always bring hiking shoes and never get to use them. My mom's caregiver is signed up till Tuesday. I'd love to take a few long hikes and enjoy a few more of Tilly's fabulous breakfasts, if it's okay?"

Demaris smiled, kind eyes regarding her. "That's why I asked."

"Anyone else up for a hike," she asked.

"Hill and I are in. What about you, Stevens?"

"Just tell me the time and place and I'll be there," their junior officer said, smiling from ear to ear.

"Boss?" she asked.

"Thanks, but any hikes I take will be close to home. Take care, everyone. Have a great weekend and I'll see you Monday morning, nine a.m., for final pack-up."

EPILOGUE

"Here we are, then," Mary Demaris called, gazing up at her ex-husband as the trio started up the front walkway.

"Hey, everyone!" A proud father opened his arms and his son ran into them. Theresa followed and gave him a more reserved embrace than her brother's. Bess waited in the open doorway, not wanting to intrude. Her presence was noted, then ignored by Mary Demaris.

Her friend, Nancy went round and opened the trunk of her car, all the while taking furtive glances at Bess. "Here, come get your bags, kids. I'm sure your dad can help. Roger, good to see you. It's been a while." She handed him two small suitcases, as Owen and Terry each grabbed a backpack.

"Nancy, nice to see you. You're looking well."

"You, too. New job must suit you. Heard about the murders. Horrible."

"What murders?" Terry asked, her eyes as big as saucers.

Mary glared at her friend. "Have you caught them?" she asked Roger.

"Yes."

"Then there's nothing to worry about, kids. Are you sure about this?" she asked, gazing from him to the figure in the open doorway.

"Of course. We're delighted to have them." He turned to smile at Bess, and she waved.

Mary nodded, then turned back to him. "Well, we'll be off, then. Terry, Owie, be good. You have my cell if anything comes up."

"We'll be fine. What time's your flight Sunday?"

"Not till six-fifteen. Nancy and I will come collect the kids around four, if that's convenient?"

"We could meet you at the airport, if that's easier, and I'm happy to drive you."

"We'll see. I'll call you Sunday morning." She hugged both the children, then hopped into the car, clearly eager to be off on her big date.

After watching the car disappear round the end of the drive, they turned and headed up the walk. "Hello," Bess called. "Welcome!"

Owen hugged her and Terry shook her hand.

"We've got your rooms all ready and can't wait to share the house with you. Are you hungry? I've got cookies and whatever you'd like to drink."

They both wanted to see their rooms, which were decorated for an eleven-year-old girl and a seven-year-old boy. Hers had a canopy bed and matching dresser, desk, and two bedside tables all painted white. Bess had purchased lovely linens with tiny pastel flowers and a matching comforter. The entire house had wide board flooring, and she had put two of her soft wool Aubusson rugs on Terry's floors on either side of the bed. The room had its own bathroom. Terry's face as she opened the door was worth all the effort of the past week to get it furnished and ready.

"Wow, Terr," her brother cried. "It's a room for a princess!"

"It's your room," Bess said, "So if you don't like it and want to change things, we can do that."

"It's perfect, thanks," Terry said shyly.

"Owen," his dad said. "You ready to see your room?"

"Yup!"

When he opened the door to his room, Owen screamed with delight. During their last visit, he had been obsessed with the *Toy Story* movies, so Bess had located cowboy sheets and comforter in Northport and had hung a few framed cowboy prints on the walls. The foot-poster bed was rough sawn pine in a honey hue with a matching dresser, desk, and bedside table. On the opposite side of the bed was a shelf displaying books, toy figures from the movie, puzzles, games, and a few trucks and cars. She had found braided rugs that complimented the colors of the room beautifully. The adjacent bathroom was tiled with deep red adobe tiles interspersed with decorative tiles of colorful animals.

"If you don't like it, we can change things, Owen," she said.

In answer, he threw his arms around her. "Thanks, Bess and Dad. It's the best room I've ever had."

Roger had brought both suitcases up, and he set them in the rooms. "Do you guys need help unpacking? The dressers are empty. There's lots of stuff in your bathrooms, too, if you forgot toothpaste or something."

"We'll do it. Thanks, Dad," Terry said as she hoisted Owen's suitcase onto his bed. "Owie, you get started. I'll unpack and come back and check, okay?"

"I can do it. Thanks, sis."

Clearly eager to get back to her room, she excused herself.

"Okay, kids, you settle in. Bess and I will be downstairs when you're ready to eat snacks or do something."

As they made their way downstairs, he whispered, "Thank you, my love."

*****

The weekend went by in a happy blur of activities—hikes across the fields to the ocean, long walks on the beach, meals at home and in the village, and spirited card and board games at night. Bess shared Roger's love of games, and they spent hours playing Go Fish, Chutes and Ladders, and Parcheesi.

They heard nothing from Mary until late Sunday morning, when Roger overheard Terry in the living room on her cell, arguing with her mother.

"No, I don't want to meet him. Too bad. We want to stay here. Dad and Bess can bring us. You said we could choose, and this is what Owen and I want. Why do you have to speak to him? Okay, hold on."

Owen and Bess out picking late raspberries from the Winthrop gardens. Roger stuck his head in his newspaper so Terry wouldn't suspect him of eavesdropping.

"Dad?"

"In the kitchen, sweetheart."

She stomped in, scowl on her face, and handed him the phone. "Mom wants to speak to you."

He grinned and took the phone. Terry stood nearby, hands on hips, waiting. "Mary? Hello. How's your weekend been?"

"Great, fine. Hate to go home. Is it really okay for you to bring the kids to the airport?"

"Absolutely. Happy to."

"That would be helpful. Jimmy and I wanted to take a drive this afternoon, maybe go to Narragansett for a beach walk before the flight. He'd like to meet the kids, but he can say hi at the airport."

"Okay. What time should we be there?"

"Five-fifteen should be fine. Everything been okay there?"

"We've had lots of fun."

"I'm glad. I suspect I'll be coming back more often."

"Anytime. We've loved having them."

"Thank you, Roger."

"For?"

"For putting up with my bullshit."

"See you later, Mary."

He handed the phone back to his daughter.

"What'd she say?"

"All set. Bess and I will take you, unless you'd rather I drive you alone?"

"No, Bess'd be fine."

Tears sprung to her eyes. He reached out, and his daughter came to sit on his lap, something she hadn't done since she was five years old. "I've missed you, Dad. So much."

"Me, too, sweetheart. But the good news is, I believe, thanks to Jimmy Pigeon, we may be seeing a lot more of each other."

They both laughed.

"Shall we go and find your brother and Bess?"

"Yes, we can't let that piggie Owen eat all the raspberries."

*****

They were quiet on the forty-five minute ride to Greene Airport. When the signs appeared for the exit, Owen asked, "When will we see you again?"

"Definitely Thanksgiving," his father replied. "But Bess and I were talking last night. Maybe we could come out to Ohio for a long weekend? Take you guys on a road trip, stay in a nice hotel with a pool? What do you think of that idea?"

"Yes!" was the chorus from the backseat.

They met Mary and Jimmy Pigeon inside the terminal, waiting to check in.

He stepped forward and extended his hand. "Hey, Roger. Been a while."

"Jimmy, good to see you. This is my wife, Bess."

"Good to meet you," he said, eyes appraising every inch of her as they shook hands. "And these must be the famous Terry and Owen I've been hearing so much about. Mom can't stop talking about you two." He bent and shook first Owen's hand, then Terry's.

"Say hi to Jimmy, kids."

The children smiled at him. As quickly as he could, Owen retreated to stand by his father.

Roger put a hand on his shoulder, gazing down at him. "Hey, buddy. We'll see you real soon. Mary, I mentioned to them the idea of us coming out for a long weekend in October, maybe taking them on an overnight, if that'd be okay with you?"

Before she could respond, Jimmy said, "Hey, maybe we could coordinate and I could come the same weekend, if you get my drift?" He winked at Roger and Bess.

"Let's talk," Mary said. "Come on, kids. Say good-bye to Dad and Jimmy. We've got to check in."

After hasty hugs all around, the three disappeared into the long line of passengers waiting to check in. Bess, Roger, and Jimmy headed out of the terminal.

As they parted company in the parking lot, Jimmy extended his hand. "Great to see you, Roger, Bess. I expect we'll be seeing more of each other in future."

"Bye. Nice to meet you," Bess said as Roger shook his hand.

*****

"So?" she asked as they drove home. "Was the weekend a success?"

"Couldn't have been better, my love, thanks to you."

"And you. You're such a wonderful dad. What did you think of Jimmy?"

"Kind of a doofus, but seems nice enough. I'll have Pete run a background check on him."

"No, you won't!"

"Just kidding, my love. Have I told you how much I love you?"

"Every moment we're together, oh husband of mine."

"Good."

Please read on to preview chapters of the first Morgan's Run Romance, *Emma's Dream*!

Acknowledgments

Thank you to my friend and neighbor, Sgt. Jason Pacheco of the Fall River, Massachusetts, Police Department, for talking with me about police procedures, and especially about the idea of a regional homicide division. Any misunderstandings in this area are entirely mine as he is always very clear and professional.

As always, I thank my dear family and friends, who are there no matter where life's travels take me. I love them all beyond words. A special thanks to my sister, Pamela, for her proofreading, and super reader, editor and proofer, Cynthia. No matter how many edits, we still find typos!

Grateful appreciation goes to the Formatting Fairies, and the unfailing good cheer and encouragement they bestow upon this writer. Special thanks to Ashley Lopez for designing the lovely covers that encourage readers to pick up each book! And of course, a huge thank you to my readers for picking up my books, for writing to tell me you love them, and for continuing to come back for more. It is heartwarming to know you are out there!

[Get my newsletter!](#)

AUTHOR'S NOTE

This book, setting, and characters are dear to me. I love writing about village life and the flawed, very human Roger Demaris. *The Silence of Memory* is the third mystery featuring Bess Dore and Roger Demaris, and I am so pleased that they are finally together. Years ago, a kind editor told me that Roger was the man for Bess, warts and all, and she was right. Thank you, Laura Jorstad.

If you liked *The Silence of Memory* and would be willing to write an Amazon review, I would very much appreciate it! In fact, I will be happy to send my first five reviewers a free copy of **another of my titles**! If you submit a review, just email me at mleeprescott@gmail.com and I will see that you receive your free copy of whichever title you would like!

If you would like to sign up for future book release alerts and occasional notices about my books, please email me at mleeprescott@gmail.com and I will add you to the list. I promise I will not share your address, nor will I flood you with emails. Do visit my website at www.mleeprescott.com to read more about my books and to hear what's next. I am really excited by my newest series, the **Morgan's Run Romances**, set in the incredible United States Southwest, another special place I visit often.

Finally, this book has been revised, proofed, and edited many, many times, but my intrepid assistants and I are human, so if you spot a typo, please email me at mleeprescott@gmail.com and I will fix it. If you'd like to know more about my other books, please scroll ahead to the next section, which is followed by sample chapters of *Emma's Dream*, Book 1 in the **Morgan's Run Romances** series.

Warm wishes,
M. Lee Prescott

ABOUT THE AUTHOR

M. Lee Prescott is the author of dozens of works of fiction for adults, young adults, and children, among them mysteries—**Prepped to Kill, Gadfly, Lost in Spindle City (Ricky Steele series), Jigsaw, A Friend of Silence**, and **In the Name of Silence**—and romances—**Widow's Island** and **Hestor's Way**. Her novel **Song of the Spirit** was a finalist in the *2014 International Digital Awards* for young adult historical fiction. Her newest contemporary romance series, **Morgan's Run,** debuts in fall 2015. Three of her nonfiction titles have been published by Heinemann, and she has published numerous articles in the field of literacy education. Lee is a professor of education at a small New England liberal arts college, where she teaches reading and writing pedagogy. Her current research focuses on mindfulness and connections to reading and writing. She regularly teaches abroad, most recently in Singapore.

Lee has lived in southern California (loved those Laguna nights!), Chapel Hill, North Carolina, and various spots in Massachusetts and Rhode Island. Currently she resides in Massachusetts on a beautiful river, where she canoes, swims, and watches the incredible variety of migratory birds and other creatures that pass by. She is the mother of two grown sons and spends lots of time with them, their beautiful wives, and her amazing grandchildren. When not teaching or writing (both of which she loves), Lee's passions revolve around family, yoga (Kripalu is a second home), swimming, cycling, sharing mindfulness with children and adults, and walking.

Lee loves to hear from readers. Visit her at http:///www.mleeprescott.com and her Facebook page (mleeprescott). Lee's email is mleeprescott@gmail.com.

NEWSLETTER SIGN-UP HERE!

Book by M. Lee Prescott include:

Mysteries

The Ricky Steele series
Book 1: Prepped to Kill
Book 2: Gadfly
Book 3: Lost in Spindle City
Book 4: Coming in 2016!

Also featuring Ricky Steele:
Jigsaw

Roger and Bess Mysteries
Book 1: A Friend of Silence
Book 2: In the Name of Silence
Book 3: The Silence of Memory

Contemporary Romance

Morgan's Run Romances (coming in fall 2015)
Emma's Dream
Lang's Return
Jeb's Promise

Well Loved Series
Widow's Island
Hestor's Way
Glass Walls (coming in 2016!)

Young Adult Historical Romance
Song of the Spirit

Excerpt from Emma's Dream Chapter 1

"This is a huge mistake," Ben Morgan muttered, his chest tightening as he steered the Range Rover over the Arizona mountain pass. "Maybe the biggest one I've made in five years."

Then he remembered it wasn't his decision. Doctor's orders propelled him eastward, away from his gorgeous new home in Santa Barbara and a rapidly expanding business, which needed his attention 24-7. The partners, his college roommates and dear friends, had assured him they could manage without him for a while, but the guilt was eating at him already. His stomach growled, but there was no place to stop in the desert that surrounded him. He would have eat in town.

As the jeep climbed the Saguaro Canyon Pass, he thought back to the previous Thursday. On the Coast Highway, headed home for a swim in the ocean after a long day at work, he was still reeling from his last encounter with Miranda, his girlfriend of two years. Their official split had been several months earlier, when he moved out of their condo and into his new home, but unfinished business, mostly financial, had necessitated one more meeting, over lunch. The parting had not been pleasant, but they still needed to work together. Miranda's law firm handled all his company's legal work, and the partners wanted to keep her on.

As he exited the restaurant, the pain started. Chalking it up to indigestion, he had hopped in the car and endeavored to ignore it. Halfway home, the pain now excruciating, he almost blacked out but was able to pull over and call 911. He told the operator he was having a heart attack.

The young whippersnapper cardiologist smiled as she leaned over his gurney. "Fascinating diagnosis, Mr. Morgan, but totally incorrect. You've had a panic attack. I'm not sure what's going on in your life right now, but whatever it is, you'd better see that it stops now, or you'll be dead before your next birthday. Thirty-two is too young to die, don't you think?"

"So, I'm crazy? Is that what you're saying?"

"No, what I'm saying is that something's going on that's triggering your physical symptoms. Are you under a lot of stress? Did anything unusual happen today?"

"Just work and the end of a romantic relationship."

She shook her head, regarding him as one might a two-year-old. "Two huge stressors. Do you have a cardiologist?"

"Why should I? I'm thirty-one, for Christ's sake."

"Right, okay. Well, then, let's pretend I'm your cardiologist. As your doctor, I am ordering you to take at least three to four months off work to decompress."

"Three to four months! Now you're the crazy one. I have a business to run and—"

"Which you won't be running for long if the stress and anxiety cause a massive heart attack. Either take time now to decompress, re-evaluate and learn ways to live your life differently, or we'll be spending a lot more time together. Do I make myself clear?"

Now, six days later, he was headed to his family's ranch in Arizona, Morgan's Run, and his enforced R & R. He laughed, wondering if returning home might actually increase his stress rather than the opposite. The Rover crested the peak, and he began his descent into the verdant valley that stretched out north and south as far as the eye could see. An orographic effect created this green, moist valley, surrounded by desert over the mountains to the east and west. In the gorgeous valley, a largely undiscovered town existed, an oasis for its roughly three thousand year-round residents and an equal number of snowbirds, tourists and wealthy vacationers, who found their way through the passes in at various points in the year.

As Ben Junior made his way into town, he passed familiar sights, largely unchanged. Nothing changed much in Saguaro. The Town Garage had a fresh coat of white paint. "Whoop-de-doo," he said aloud, making a mental note to drop the Rover off for servicing soon.

As he turned right on Main and headed toward Gracie's Diner, a horn blared and the clunker in front of him screeched to a stop. Ben braked, but not in time to stop the Rover before it tapped the rear of the clunker. Ben swore under his breath and backed up, pulling over to park at the curb. As he did, the clunker's driver leaped from her car, screaming and waving her arms. He shook his head. Foolish woman had left her heap in the middle of the street. Tall and slender, she wore Jackie O. sunglasses, a baseball cap pulled low on her forehead, a faded cotton shirt over blue jeans, and cowboy boots, the uniform for nearly every female rancher in the valley.

"Geez, Toto," he muttered, patting the Rover's seat. "We're not in Kansas anymore."

As she approached the Rover, Ben noticed her jeans hugged every curve, full breasts not quite obscured by the baggy shirt. He couldn't see her face, but he had to admit the rest of the package was intriguing and also vaguely familiar. He approached as she bent to survey the clunker's bumper.

"What's the matter with you?" she screamed, walking in circles, arms still flailing. "Oh, my God, oh, my God, what am I going to do?"

Ben stared at her back, astounded at what was clearly a huge overreaction. The clunker was fine, hardly a scratch on it, although it would be hard to tell with all the other dings. Then, just as quickly as it started, the fire went out and she flopped down to sit on the curb, head between her legs, sobbing.

"Hey, hey, it's not that bad, is it? We hardly touched each other. No harm done." He sat beside her, wondering whether he should pat her on the shoulder. Immediately she quieted and looked up at him.

"Oh, my God. This just gets better and better. It figures."

Ben Morgan, the one person she expected never to see again, sitting beside her in the middle of Main Street. Could things get any worse? She leaned forward, hiding her face, wondering whether he'd go away if she sat there long enough.

"Maggie? Is that little Maggie Williams? After five years, I'm in town less than a minute and the first person I bump into is you."

Maggie groaned and buried her head deeper, praying this was all a bad dream. If she hadn't had to make a quick run to the bank, she'd be at work in the cool, dark stables.

"Please just go. I'm fine."

She could feel his heat, his nearness rattling her to her core. A part of her longed to lean against him and draw comfort and strength from his warmth, but the wiser half screamed *danger*. She kept still, hoping he would disappear.

"You don't seem fine. Look, I'm sorry." Ben placed a hand on her shoulder. It sent shivers of warmth all the way to her toes. "And I'm not leaving until I'm sure you're okay."

Oh, no you don't. Maggie stood and shook herself, stepping away from his electric touch. She put on her sunglasses. Another second near him and she feared she might actually swoon. His soft chestnut eyes regarded her with obvious concern. Although he looked tired and thin, Ben Morgan was still drop-dead gorgeous, in faded jeans and sneakers, his broad shoulders straining the seams of a worn Stanford tee shirt.

"I'm fine, really. It's been a crazy day and you caught me at a bad time. I'm sorry I overreacted."

Ben watched her, wondering why a fender kiss had caused so much distress. "Can I give you a lift somewhere?"

"No, of course not! I mean, thanks, but I'm okay now. Got to get back to work."

"Where's that?"

"Sorry, I'm really late. Good to see you again. Take care."

She hopped into her car and drove away before he could utter another word.

What the hell was that? Ben thought back to his one memorable night with Maggie Williams. They had both left Saguaro shortly after that night, but a part of him always wondered if there was something more to explore with his brother Kyle's beautiful classmate. While he had pushed thoughts of her and their one night of passionate sex from his mind, as he watched her drive away, Ben realized that he had spent five years comparing every woman he met to Maggie Williams. His stomach growled, and he shook his head. *Enough, time to eat!* He left the Rover and walked the three blocks to Gracie's.

CHAPTER 2

Noon rush over, Gracie's was empty except for one booth occupied by a family of four savoring the last spoonfuls of a Gracie Gila Monster. The diner's signature sundae was made with Gracie's secret chocolate sauce, vanilla ice cream, and hot toffee sauce, topped with whipped cream, then sprinkled liberally with crumbled peanut butter cups. Ben was tempted to forgo lunch and go for a Gila but decided on a portabella burger instead. With a nod to the family, he sidled up and took a stool at the counter.

A young freckle-faced redhead, ponytail wagging, bounced up, flashing him a smile that lit up the room. "Hi, sir. Can I take your order?"

"Hi, yourself. I don't know you. Are you new in town?"

She regarded him quizzically with lots of eyelash batting. "No, but you are. I'd remember you. Been here three years. I'm a student at U of A, but summers I come up to Saguaro instead goin' home to Yuma. Too hot. My dad works down there. Just passing through?"

Ben gave her the hundred-watt smile that made most women swoon. She was no exception. "You could say that. Name's Ben."

"I'm Stacy. What can I get you, Ben?"

"Iced tea and a portabella burger, lettuce, tomato, and lots of Gracie's burger sauce."

"Comin' right up."

Ben watched her disappear into the kitchen, relieved that he had not yet met anyone he knew. He wanted to surprise his parents.

Well—he *had* met someone, he mused, remembering the curvaceous, lush-lipped Maggie Williams. It had been all he could do not to sweep her into his arms and kiss away those tears. Once again, he wondered at the subconscious torch he had been carrying for her. And what was with her behavior? *Who falls apart and sobs uncontrollably over a bumper tap?*

As he savored the last bite of his burger, Gracie emerged from the kitchen. "Still a vegetarian, I see. Crime in God's country."

Ben stood as she came around the counter to grab him in a bear hug. At six-four, he had her by a few inches, but Gracie was at least six feet herself, a towering figure in a grease-covered apron and frayed jeans, her wiry black hair streaked with gray, cut short, and sticking out at odd angles.

"How's my desert goddess? Have you missed me? You look younger than when I left."

"Tush." She waved her hand, clearly pleased at the compliment. "Always were the biggest liar from here to Albuquerque. Are you home to stay?"

"No, just a break from the rat race."

"Your folks must be thrilled. Can't believe they won't be angling for you to stay on, what with your dad slowing down and your brothers scattered hither and yon."

"Is Dad okay?"

Gracie gave him a measured look before answering. "Course he is. Strong as an ox, but he's not twenty-five anymore. Could use the help, I'm sure."

"Gracie, this is me. Has something happened to Dad?"

"He's fine, dearie. Had a minor dust-up last year, but from your expression, I guess he didn't tell you about it. Not my place. Let him or your mom fill you in."

He stared at her for a moment or two, knowing he would not get another word out of her. "If you could keep my arrival quiet till I see them, I'd be grateful, Gracie."

Ben went for his wallet, suddenly anxious to be home.

Gracie waved her hand. "Not on your life! Put that city money away and git up there and say howdy-do to your folks."

He leaned over and pecked her cheek. "Thanks, Gracie. Great to see you."

"Good to have you home where you belong," she said, gently nudging him toward the door. "Hope it's for good."

CHAPTER 3

Maggie drove through the main gate of Morgan's Run and pulled into her usual spot behind the stables. She killed the engine and drew out her cell phone. When her father answered, she breathed a sigh of relief.

"How's my angel?"

"Good as gold. What's the matter, sweetie? You sound upset."

"Nothing, just wanted to check in."

"She's napping. Should I phone when she wakes so you can say hello?"

"No, I'll see her in a few hours."

"Mags, what is it? What's happened?"

"Ben Morgan's back."

"Oh? Bump into each other, did you?"

"You could say that. We had a fender bender, right on Main Street."

"You okay?"

"Yes, just embarrassed. When it happened, I freaked out. Made a total fool of myself, crying and wailing over a minor bumper tap. Thank goodness no one else was around."

"Glad you're okay. You gonna tell him about Emma?"

A truck drove up beside her and Maggie spied Jeb, her assistant.

"Dad, I gotta go. See you tonight."

"Take care, honey."

Maggie waved to her assistant. "Hey, Jeb. You ready to tackle Tabasco?"

She referred to a spirited mustang they were training, the size of a small draft horse. Soon his rider, a Border Patrol agent, would join them to participate in the final weeks of training. Then horse and rider would return to Nogales as a team, ready to keep watch in the mountains along the border.

"Ready when you are. You okay, Boss? You look a little green around the gills."

"Fine, just tired."

"How's my little cutie pie doin'?"

"Full of it, curious, into everything, just like most four-year-olds. She keeps Dad busy."

"How's the therapy going?"

"Not much progress. She's just outgrown her third wheelchair."

"Wow, has it been that long?"

Maggie nodded. The sadness since the accident sometimes overwhelmed her, etching new lines across her brow and haunting her dreams. Afraid to be far from her phone, she watched the clock until it was time to head home. It wasn't that she disliked the work. Maggie loved training horses, assisting with the day-to-day running of Morgan Run's stables, but she worried continuously about Emma. Two years ago, the toddler had just learned to walk when her legs had been knocked out from under her, paralyzed when their car had been broadsided by a drunk driver.

Hands on hips, she stared at Jeb, who seemed a million miles away. "Are you coming or not?"

"Sorry, Boss!"

He fell in step beside her as they headed for Tabasco's stall.

Get *Emma's Dream*!

9 780099 128558 7